Joe's Luck

BY

Horatio Alger, Jr.

Reprinted by:

**James Stevenson Publisher
1500 Oliver Road, Suite K-109
Fairfield, CA 94533
707-469-0237
jimstevenson@jspub.com
Fax: 508-374-7762**

James Stevenson Publisher
copyright © 2002
Joe's Luck cover design

ISBN 1-885852-21-5

PREFACE

The story of "Joe's Luck" is laid at the time of the Gold Fever in California and has for its hero a young boy of excellent character and noble qualities. The story tells how he makes his way from New York to California, by boat, and then wins what seems to him a fortune.

Many regarded his success as the result of luck, but it was really the result of his industry and perseverance coupled with his remarkable faculty for making friends.

Printed in the United States of America

CHAPTER I

INTRODUCES JOE

"Come here, you Joe, and be quick about it!"

The boy addressed, a stout boy of fifteen, with an honest, sun-browned face, looked calmly at the speaker.

"What's wanted?" he asked.

"Brush me off, and don't be all day about it!" said Oscar Norton, impatiently.

Joe's blue eyes flashed indignantly at the tone of the other.

"You can brush yourself off," he answered.

"What's up, I wonder? Ain't you our servant?"

"I am not your servant, though your father is my employer."

"Are you going to brush me off?"

"No."

Oscar, much incensed, went to his father to report Joe's insubordination. While he is absent, a few words of explanation will enlighten the reader as to Joe's history and present position.

Joe Mason was alone in the world. A year previous he had lost his father, his only remaining parent, and when the father's affairs were settled and funeral expenses paid, there was found to be just five dollars left, which was expended for clothing for Joe.

JOE'S LUCK

In this emergency, Major Norton, a farmer and capitalist, offered to provide Joe with board and clothes and three months' schooling in the year in return for his services. As nothing else offered, Joe accepted, but would not bind himself for any length of time.

Now, there were two disagreeable things in Joe's new place. The first was the parsimony of Major Norton, who was noted for his stingy disposition, and the second was the overbearing manners of Oscar, who lost no opportunity to humiliate Joe and tyrannize over him so far as Joe's independent spirit would allow. It happened, therefore, that Joe was compelled to work hard, while the promised clothing was of the cheapest and shabbiest description. He was compelled to go to school in patched shoes and a ragged suit, which hurt his pride as he compared himself with Oscar, who was carefully and even handsomely dressed. Parsimonious as his father was, he was anxious that his only boy should appear to advantage.

On the very day on which our story begins Oscar had insulted Joe in a way which excited our hero's bitter indignation.

Joe, who was a general favorite on account of his good looks and gentlemanly manners, and in spite of his shabby attire, was walking home with Annie Raymond, the daughter of the village physician, when Oscar came up.

He was himself secretly an admirer of the young lady, but had never received the least encouragement from her. It made him angry to see his

JOE'S LUCK

father's drudge walking on equal terms with his own favorite, and his coarse nature prompted him to insult his enemy.

"Miss Raymond," he said, lifting his hat, mockingly, "I congratulate you on the beau you have picked up."

Annie Raymond fully appreciated his meanness, and answered calmly:

"I accept your congratulations, Mr. Norton."

This answer made Oscar angry, and led him to go further than he otherwise would.

"You must be hard up for an escort when you accept such a ragamuffin as Joe Mason."

"Oscar Norton, do you mean to insult Miss Raymond or me?" he demanded.

"I certainly don't mean to insult Miss Raymond, but I wonder at her taste in choosing my father's hired boy to walk with."

"I am not responsible to you for my choice, Oscar Norton," said Annie Raymond, with dignity. "If my escort is poorly dressed, it is not his fault, nor do I think the less of him for it."

"If your father would dress me better, I should be very glad of it," said Joe. "If I am a ragamuffin it is his fault."

"I'll report that to him," said Oscar, maliciously.

"Suppose we go on," said Annie Raymond.

And they walked on, leaving Oscar discomfited and mortified.

Oscar would have liked to despise Annie Raymond, but it was out of his power. She was undoubtedly the belle of the school, and he would have been proud

JOE'S LUCK

to receive as much notice from her as she freely accorded to Joe. But the young lady had a mind and a will of her own, and she had seen too much to dislike in Oscar to regard him with favor, even if he were the son of a rich man, while she had the good sense and discrimination to see that Joe, despite his ragged garb, possessed sterling good qualities.

When Oscar got home he sought his father.

"Father," said he, "I heard Joe complaining to Annie Raymond that you didn't dress him decently."

"What does the boy mean?" he said.

"He should be dressed as well as I am," said Oscar.

"I don't want folks to talk," said the major, who was sensitive to public opinion. "Don't you think his clothes are good enough?"

"Of course they are; but I'll tell you what, father," said Oscar, with a sudden idea, "you know that suit of mine that I got stained with acid?"

"Yes, Oscar," said the major, gravely. "I ought to remember it. It cost me thirty-four dollars, and you spoiled it by your carelessness."

"Suppose you give that to Joe?" suggested Oscar.

"He's a good deal larger than you. It wouldn't fit him, and, besides, it's stained."

"I dare say Joe won't like the idea of wearing it, but a boy in his position has no right to be proud."

"Of course not," returned the major, his ruling passion gratified by the prospect of saving the price of a suit. "When Joseph comes home—at any rate, after he is through with his chores—you may tell him to come in to me."

"All right, sir."

JOE'S LUCK

Before Oscar remembered this message, the scene narrated at the commencement of the chapter occured. On his way to complain to his father, he recollected the message, and, retracing his steps, said to Joe:

"My father wants to see you right off."

This was a summons which Joe felt it his duty to obey. He accordingly bent his steps to the room where Major Norton usually sat.

"Oscar tells me you wish to see me, sir," said Joe, as he entered the presence of his pompous employer.

"Oscar tells me that you are not satisfied with the clothes I have given you."

"He has told you the truth, Major Norton."

"Here is a suit of Oscar's," he said, "which is quite whole and almost new. Oscar only wore it a month. It cost me *thirty-four dollars!*" said the major, impressively.

He held it up, and Joe recognized it at once.

"Isn't it the suit Oscar got stained?" he asked, abruptly.

"Ahem! yes, it is a *little* stained, but that doesn't injure the texture of the cloth."

As he held it up the entire suit seemed to have been sprinkled with acid, which had changed the color in large patches in different parts. The wearer would be pretty sure to excite an unpleasant degree of attention.

Joe pulled off his coat and put on the stained one. The sleeves were from two to three inches too short, and it was so far from meeting in front, on account of his being much broader than Oscar, that his shoulders seemed drawn back to meet each other behind.

"It doesn't exactly fit," said the major, "but it can be let out easily. I will send it to Miss Pearce, the village tailoress, to fix over for you."

"Thank you, Mr. Norton," said Joe in a decided tone, "but I hope you won't go to that expense, for I shall not be willing to wear it under any circumstances."

"You can go, Joseph," said Major Norton in a tone of annoyance. "I did not expect to find you so unreasonable. If you do not chose to take what I offer you, you will have to go without."

"Very well, sir."

Joe's work was done, and being left free to do as he liked, he strolled over to the village store.

CHAPTER II

THE RETURNED CALIFORNIAN

The village store in the evening was a sort of village clubhouse, where not only the loungers, but a better class, who desired to pass the evening socially, were wont to congregate. About the center of the open space was a large box-stove which in winter was kept full of wood, oftimes getting red-hot, and around this sat the villagers. Some on wooden chairs, some on a wooden settee with a broken back which was ranged on one side.

JOE'S LUCK

Joe frequently came here in the evening to pass a social hour and kill time. At the house of Major Norton he had no company.

When Joe entered the store he found the usual company present, but with one addition.

This was Seth Larkin, who had just returned from California, whither he had gone eighteen months before, and was, of course, an object of great attention.

It was in the fall of the year 1851, and so in the early days of California.

Seth was speaking as Joe entered.

"Is there gold in California?" repeated Seth, apparently in answer to a question. "I should say there was. Why, it's chock full of it. People haven't begun to find out the richness of the country. It's the place for a poor man to go if he wants to become rich. What's the prospects here? I ask any one of you. A man may go working and plodding from one year's end to another, and not have ten dollars at the end of it. There's some here that know that I speak the truth."

"How much better can a man do in California?" asked Daniel Tompkins.

"Well, Dan," said Seth, "it depends on the kind of man he is. If he's a man like you, that spends his money for rum as fast as he gets it, I should say it's just as well to stay here. But if he's willing to work hard, and to put by half he makes, he's sure to do well, and he may get rich. Why, I knew a man that landed in California the same day that I did, went up to the mines, struck a vein,

JOE'S LUCK

and—well, how much do you think that man is worth to-day?"

"A thousand dollars?" suggested Dan Tompkins.

"Two thousand?" guessed Sam Stone.

"Well, boys, I s'pose I may as well tell you, and you may b'lieve it or not, just as you like. That man is worth twenty thousand dollars to-day."

There was a chorus of admiring ejaculations.

"What made you come home, Seth, if you were gettin' on so well?" inquired one.

"That's a fair question," said Seth, "and I'm willin' to answer it. It was because of the rheumatics. I had 'em powerful bad at the mines, and I've come home to kinder recuperate, if that's the right word. But I'm goin' back ag'in, you may bet high on that."

"How much does it cost to go out there?" asked Dan Tompkins.

"More money than you can scare together, Dan. First-class nigh on to three hundred dollars, I believe."

"You can go second-class for a good deal less, and you can go round the Horn pretty cheap," continued Seth.

"How far away is Californy?" inquired Sam Stone.

"By way of the Isthmus it must be as much as six thousand miles, and it's twice as fur, I reckon, round the Horn. I don't exactly know the distance."

"Then it's further away than Europe," said Joe, who had been listening with eager interest.

"Of course it is," said Seth. "Why, that's Joe Mason, isn't it? How you have grown since I saw you."

JOE'S LUCK

"Do you think I have?" said Joe, pleased with the assurance. "Is there any chance for a boy in California, Mr. Larkin?"

"Well, there's a chance for a boy if he's smart, but he's got to work."

"I should be willing to do that."

"Then if you ever get the chance it won't do you any harm to try your luck."

"How much did you say it costs to get there?"

"Well, maybe you could get there for a hundred dollars if you wasn't particular how you went."

A hundred dollars! It might as well have been ten thousand as far as Joe was concerned. He received no money wages, nor was he likely to as long as he remained in the major's employ.

Joe sighed as he thought how far away was the prospect of his being able to go to California.

He walked home slowly, dreaming of the goldfields on the other side of the continent and wishing he were there.

The next day was Saturday. There was no school, but this did not lighten Joe's labors, as he was kept at work on the farm all day.

He was in the barn when Deacon Goodwin, a neighbor, drove up.

Oscar was standing in front of the house whittling out a cane from a stick he had cut in the woods.

"Is Joe Mason at home?" he inquired.

Oscar looked up in surprise. Why should the deacon want Joe Mason.

"Probably he is in the barn," said Oscar, indifferently.

JOE'S LUCK

"Will you call him? I want to see him on business."

Oscar hesitated. Finally he decided to go.

He opened the barn door and called out:

"Here, you Joe! Deacon Goodwin wants you out at the gate."

Joe was as much surprised as Oscar.

"I'll come," he said.

He followed Oscar to the front of the house and bade the deacon good-morning.

"Oscar tells me you want to see me," he said.

"Yes, Joe. Do you remember your Aunt Susan?"

"My mother's aunt?"

"Yes. I reckon by her age she couldn't have been your own aunt. Well, she's dead. The old lady had a small pension," continued the deacon, "that just about kept her, but she managed to save a little out of it. When the funeral expenses were paid, it was found that there were fifty-six dollars and seventy-five cents over."

"What's going to be done with it?" he inquired.

"She's left it to you," was the unexpected reply. "You was the nearest relation she had, and it was her wish that whatever was left should go to you."

Joe's eyes sparkled with pleasure. He had never possessed five dollars at a time in his life, and the legacy, small as it was, seemed to him a fortune.

"I'm very much obliged to her," he said. "I didn't expect anything. I had almost forgotten I had a great-aunt."

"The money has been sent to me, Joe," continued the deacon. "I'm ready to pay it over to you when you want it. Do you want me to keep it for you?"

"I don't know," said Joe; "I haven't had time to think. I'll come round to-night and see you about it if you'll be at home. I should like to have you keep it till then."

"Very well, Joseph. G'lang, Dobbin!" and the deacon started his old horse, who had completed his quarter-century, along the road.

Oscar had listened not without interest to the conversation. Though he was the son of a rich man, he had not at command so large a sum as his father's hired boy had fallen heir to. On the whole, he respected Joe rather more than when he was altogether penniless.

"You're in luck, Joe," said he, more graciously than usual.

"Yes," said Joe. "It's very unexpected."

On the way to the deacon's Joe fell in with Seth Larkin.

"Well, my boy, where are you bound?" asked Seth.

"To collect my fortune," said Joe.

Seth asked for an explanation, and received it.

"I'm glad for you, and I wish it were more," he said.

"Yes; if it were enough I would go to California."

"You really want to go?"

"Yes. I suppose fifty dollars wouldn't be enough?"

"No, it wouldn't," said Seth, "but I'll tell you what you could do. Go to New York, and keep yourself there till you got a chance to work your passage, as a cabin-boy, round the Horn."

JOE'S LUCK

"So I might," said Joe, brightening up.

"Well, if you decide to go, come round and see me to-morrow, and I'll give you the best advice I can."

"Thank you, Seth."

Here they reached the deacon's house, and Joe went in.

The deacon opposed Joe's plan, but in vain. Our hero had made up his mind. Finally the old man counted out the money, and Joe put it in an old wallet.

The next thing was to give Major Norton warning of his desire to leave him. He found the major at home and obtained an interview.

"Major Norton," said Joe, coming to the point at once, "I should like you to get another boy in my place."

"What, Joe?" exclaimed the major. "Why what's come now?"

"I am going to leave town."

"Where are you going?" asked his employer.

"First to New York, and afterward to California, if I can get there."

"Well, I declare! But you haven't got any money."

"I have almost sixty dollars."

"Oh, yes; Oscar told me. You'd better stay here, and let me keep it for you."

"No, sir; I have made up my mind. I want to start Monday morning."

"You'll come back in a month without a cent in your pocket."

"If I do, I'll go to work again for you, if you'll take me."

JOE'S LUCK

Monday morning came. Clad in his Sunday suit of cheap and rough cloth, Joe stood on the platform at the depot. The cars came up, he jumped aboard and his heart beat with exultation as he reflected that he had taken the first step toward the Land of Gold.

CHAPTER III

AT THE COMMERCIAL HOTEL

Joe had never been to New York, and when he arrived, the bustle and confusion at first bewildered him.

He made his way out of the crowd, and paused at the corner of the next street for reflection. Finally he stopped at an apple and peanut stand, and as a matter of policy purchased an apple.

"I am from the country," he said, "and I want to find a cheap hotel. Can you recommend one to me?"

"Yes," said the peanut merchant. "I know of one where they charge a dollar a day."

The requisite directions were given. It was the Commercial Hotel, located in a down-town street very near the Battery. Joe lost his way once or twice, but he had a tongue in his head and was soon set right.

He walked up to the desk, on which was spread out wide open the hotel register. Rather a dissipated-looking clerk stood behind the counter picking his teeth.

JOE'S LUCK

"Good-morning, sir," said Joe, politely. "Can you give me a room?"

"I guess so, my son. Haven't you got any baggage?"

"Here it is."

"Is that all you've got?"

"Yes."

"Then you'll have to pay in advance. That wouldn't be security for your bill."

"All right," said Joe. "I'll pay a day in advance."

"You may put down your name."

Joe took the pen and made this entry in the register:

"Joseph Mason, Oakville, New Jersey."

A freckle-faced boy was summoned, provided with the key of No. 161, and Joe was directed to follow him.

They went up-stairs until Joe wondered when they were going to stop. Finally the boy paused at the top floor.

Joe found himself in a room about ten feet by six, with a small window, a single bed, and a discolored washstand supporting a cracked bowl and a pitcher which had lost its handle. There was a wooden chair and dressing-table, and these were about all that the room could conveniently hold.

"There you are. You wouldn't like some hot water for shaving, would you?" asked the boy with a grin.

"You can have some put on to heat and I'll order it when my beard is grown," said Joe good-naturedly.

"All right. I'll tell 'em to be sure and have it ready in two or three years."

JOE'S LUCK

"That will be soon enough. You'd better order some for yourself at the same time."

"Oh, that ain't necessary. I get in hot water every day."

The freckle-faced boy disappeared, and Joe sat down on the bed to reflect a little on his position and plans.

So here he was in New York, and on the way to California, too—that is, he hoped so.

He washed his hands and face and went downstairs. He found that dinner was just ready, and he went into the dining-room and ate with a country boy's appetite. It was not a luxurious meal, but compared with the major's rather frugal table there was a great variety and luxury. Joe did justice to it.

"Now," thought Joe, after dinner was over, "the first thing for me to find out is when the California steamer starts and what is the lowest price I can go for."

In the bar-room Joe found a file of two of the New York daily papers, and began to search diligently the advertising columns in search of the advertisement of the California steamers.

At last he found it.

The steamer was to start in three days. Apply for passage and any information at the company's offices.

"I'll go right down there and find out whether I've got money enough to take me," Joe decided.

The office of the steamer was on the wharf from which it was to start. Joe made his way to the office, which he entered.

JOE'S LUCK

"Is this the office of the California steamer, sir?"

"Yes."

"What is the lowest price for passage?"

"A hundred dollars for the steerage."

When Joe heard this his heart sunk within him. It seemed to be the death-blow to his hopes. He had but fifty dollars or thereabouts, and there was no chance whatever of getting the extra fifty. But Joe didn't like to give it up. He resolved to make one effort more.

"Couldn't I pay you fifty dollars now and the rest as soon as I can earn it in California?" he pleaded.

"We don't do business in that way," said the stout man, decisively.

Of course there was no more to be said. Joe left the office not a little disheartened.

The afternoon slipped away almost without Joe's knowledge. He walked about here and there, gazing with curious eyes at the streets and warehouses and passing vehicles, and thinking what a lively place New York was, and how different life was in the metropolis from what it had been to him in the quiet country town which had hitherto been his home. Somehow it seemed to wake Joe up and excite his ambition, to give him a sense of power which he had never felt before.

He got back to the hotel in time for supper, and with an appetite nearly as good as he had at dinner.

When supper was over he went into the public room of the Commercial Hotel and took up a paper to read. There was a paragraph about California and some recent discoveries there, which he read

JOE'S LUCK.

with avidity. The more he heard and read about this golden land the more disappointed he was that he could not go there by the very next steamer.

Though Joe was not aware of it, he was closely observed by a dark-complexioned man, dressed in rather a flashy manner, who sat a few feet from him. When our hero laid down the paper, this man commenced a conversation.

"I take it you are a stranger in the city, my young friend," he observed in an affable manner.

"Yes, sir," answered Joe. "I only arrived this morning."

"Indeed! May I ask from what part of the country you come?"

"From Oakville, New Jersey."

"So you have come to the city to try your luck, have you?"

"Yes, sir—that is, I don't mean to stay in New York. I want to go to California."

"Oh, I see—to the gold-diggings. A remarkable country, California. When do you expect to start?"

"I may not be able to go at all. I haven't got money enough to buy a ticket."

"You have got some money, haven't you?" asked the stranger, seeming interested.

"Yes—I have fifty dollars, but I went to the office today, and find that a hundred dollars is the lowest price for a ticket."

"Don't be discouraged, my young friend," said the stranger in the most friendly manner. "I am aware that the ordinary charge for a steerage ticket is one hundred dollars, but exceptions are sometimes made."

JOE'S LUCK

"I don't think they will make one in my case," said Joe. "I told the agent I would agree to pay the other half as soon as I earned it, but he said he didn't do business in that way."

"Of course. You are a stranger to him, don't you see? That makes all the difference in the world. Now, I happen to be personally acquainted with him—in fact, we used to go to school together. I am sure he would do me a favor. Just give me the fifty dollars, and I'll warrant I'll get the ticket for you."

Joe was not wholly without caution, and the thought of parting with his money to a stranger didn't strike him favorably. Not that he had any doubts as to his new friend's integrity, but it didn't seem business-like.

"Can't I go with you to the office?" he suggested.

"I'll tell you what—you needn't hand me the money, provided you agree to take the ticket off my hands at fifty dollars if I secure it."

"Certainly I will, and be very thankful to you besides," said Joe.

"I always like to help young men along," said the stranger, benevolently. "I'll see about it to-morrow. Now, where can I meet you—say at four o'clock in the afternoon?"

"In this room. How will that do?"

"Perfectly. I am sure I can get the ticket for you."

Punctually at four the next day the stranger entered the room where Joe was already awaiting him.

"Have you succeeded?" asked Joe, eagerly.

The stranger nodded.

JOE'S LUCK

"Let us go to your room, my young friend, and complete our business."

"All right, sir."

Joe got his key and led the way up-stairs to room No. 161.

"Here is the ticket," said the stranger.

He produced a large card, which read thus:

CALIFORNIA STEAMSHIP COMPANY

The Bearer is Entitled to One Steerage Passage
from
NEW YORK TO SAN FRANCISCO

STEAMER COLUMBUS

Below this was printed the name of the stranger.

Joe paid over the money joyfully.

"I am very much obliged to you," he said, gratefully.

"Don't mention it," said the stranger, pocketing the fifty dollars. "Good-day! Sorry to leave you, but I am to meet a gentleman at five."

He went down-stairs and left Joe alone.

CHAPTER IV

JOE'S LUCK CHANGES

"How lucky I have been," thought Joe, in the best of spirits. "There wasn't one chance in ten of my succeeding, and yet I have succeeded. Everything has turned out right. If I hadn't met this man I couldn't have got a ticket at half-price. It was certainly very kind to take so much trouble for a stranger."

Joe counted over his money and found that he could barely scrape through. After paying his hotel expenses he would have a dollar left over. This would be rather a small sum to start with in California, but Joe didn't trouble himself much about that. If he only got there he felt that he should get along somehow.

He had a whole day to explore the city, and he decided to make the most of it. He wanted to carry away with him a good idea of New York, for it was uncertain when he would visit the city again.

The next day, about two hours before the time of sailing, Joe went down to the wharf of the California steamer.

As he was going on board a man stopped him.

"Have you got a ticket?" he asked.

"Yes, sir," said Joe, "a steerage ticket. There it is," and he confidently produced the ticket which he had bought for fifty dollars.

"Where did you get this?" asked the man.

JOE'S LUCK

"From a friend of mine," said Joe.

"How much did you pay for it?"

"Fifty dollars."

"Then you have lost your money, for it is a bogus ticket. You can't travel on it."

Joe stared at the other in blank dismay. The earth seemed to be sinking under him. He realized that he had been outrageously swindled, and that he was further from going to California than ever.

The intelligence that his ticket was valueless came to Joe like a thunder-bolt from a clear sky. The minute before he was in high spirits—his prospects seemed excellent and his path bright. Now he seemed to have no future. He felt like a shipwrecked sailor, who is cast upon an uninhabited island, utterly without resources.

"What shall I do?" he ejaculated.

"I can't tell you," said the officer. "One thing is clear, you can't go to California on that ticket."

Poor Joe! For a moment hope was dead within his breast. He was certainly placed in a very difficult position. He had but one dollar left, and that was only half the amount necessary to carry him back to the country village where we found him at the commencement of our story. Even if he were able to go back, he felt he would be ashamed to report the loss of his money. The fact that he had allowed himself to be swindled mortified him not a little. He would never hear the last of it if he returned to Oakville.

"Wouldn't I like to get hold of the man that sold me the ticket."

JOE'S LUCK

He had hardly given mental expression to this wish when it was gratified. The very man passed him, and was about to cross the gang-plank into the steamer. Joe's eyes flashed, and he sprung forward and seized the man by the arm.

The swindler's countenance changed when he recognized Joe, but he quickly decided upon his course.

"What do you want, Johnny?" he asked, composedly.

"What do I want? I want my fifty dollars back."

"I don't know what you are talking about," said he.

"You sold me a bogus ticket for fifty dollars," said Joe, stoutly. "Here it is. Take it back and give me my money."

"The boy must be crazy," said the swindler.

"Did you sell him that ticket?" inquired the officer.

"Never saw him before in the whole course of my life," persisted the man, with brazen effrontery.

"Ain't you mistaken, boy?" asked the officer.

"No, sir. This is the very man. I'm willing to swear to it."

"Have you any business here?" asked the officer.

"Yes," said the man, I've taken a steerage ticket to San Francisco. Here it is."

"All right. Go in."

He tore himself from Joe's grasp, and went on board the steamer.

Joe fell back, because he was obliged to. He looked around hoping that he might somewhere see a policeman, for he wanted to punish the scoundrel to whom he owed his unhappiness and loss. But, as

JOE'S LUCK

frequently happens, when an officer is wanted, none is to be seen.

Joe did not leave the wharf. Time was not of much value to him, and he decided that he might as well remain and see the steamer start on which he had fondly hoped to be a passenger. Then he would realize that he was finally cut off from the chance of going to California, and could think over his plans at his leisure, for of leisure he was likely to have an unlimited supply.

Meanwhile the preparations for departure went steadily forward. Trunks arrived and were conveyed on board, passengers accompanied by their friends came, and all was hurry and bustle.

Two young men, handsomely dressed and apparently possessed of larger means than the great majority of the passengers, got out of a hack, and paused close to where Joe was standing.

"Dick," said one, "I'm really sorry you are not going with me. I shall feel awfully lonely without you."

"I am very much disappointed, Charlie, but duty will keep me at home. My father's sudden alarming sickness has broken up all my plans. If I should go, I should make myself miserable all the way with the thought of what might happen."

"Yes, Dick, under the circumstances of course you can't go."

"If my father should recover in a few weeks, I will come out and join you, Charlie."

"I hope you may be able to, Dick. By the way, how about your ticket?"

JOE'S LUCK

"I shall have to lose it unless the company will give me another in place of it."

"They ought to do it."

"Yes, but they are rather stiff about it. If there were more time, I might be able to find a purchaser, but, as you know my father was only taken sick last night. I would sell it, though it is a first-class ticket, for a hundred dollars."

Joe heard this and his heart beat high with excitement.

He pressed forward and said, eagerly:

"Will you sell it to me for that?"

The young man addressed as Dick looked in surprise at the poorly dressed boy who had addressed him.

"Do you want to go to California?" he asked.

"Yes, sir," said Joe; "I am very anxious to go."

"Do I understand you to offer a hundred dollars for my ticket?"

"Yes, sir, but I can't pay you now."

"When do you expect to be able to pay me, then?"

"Not till I've earned the money in California," Joe admitted, candidly.

"Have you thought before of going?" inquired the young man addressed as Charlie.

"Yes, sir. Until an hour ago I thought that it was all arranged that I should go. I came down here and found that the ticket I had bought was a bogus one and that I had been swindled out of my money."

"That was a mean trick," said Dick Scudder, indignantly. "Do you know the man that cheated you?"

"Yes, he is on board the steamer. He took my money and bought a ticket for himself."

"How much money have you got left?"

"A dollar."

"Only a dollar? And you are not afraid to land in California with this sum?"

"No, sir. I shall go to work at once. I shan't mind the kind of work. I will do anything."

"Charlie," said Dick, turning to his friend, "I will do as you say. Are you willing to take this boy into your state-room in my place?"

"Yes," said Charles Folsom, promptly. "He looks like a good boy. I accept him as my room-mate."

"All right," said the other. "My boy, what is your name?"

"Joe Mason."

"Well, Joe, here is my ticket. If fortune prospers you and you are ever able to pay a hundred dollars for this ticket, you may pay it to my friend, Charles Folsom. Now, I advise you both to be getting aboard, as it is nearly time for the steamer to sail. I won't go on with you, Charlie, as I must go back to my father's bedside."

"Good-by, sir. God bless you!" said Joe, gratefully.

"Good-by, Joe, and good luck!"

As they went over the gang plank the officer, recognizing Joe, said roughly:

"Stand back, boy. Didn't I tell you you couldn't go aboard without a ticket?"

"Here is my ticket," said Joe.

"A first-class ticket!" exclaimed the officer in

amazement. "Where in the world did you get it?"

"I bought it," answered Joe.

"I shall go to California after all!" thought our hero, exultingly.

CHAPTER V

THE FIRST DAY ON BOARD

"We will look up our state-room first, Joe," said his new friend. "It ought to be a good one, for I engaged it some time in advance."

The state-room proved to be No. 16, very well located and spacious for a state-room. But to Joe it seemed very small for two persons. He was an inexperienced traveler and did not understand that life on board ship is widely different from life on shore. His companion had been to Europe and was used to steamer-life.

"I think, Joe," said he, "that I shall put you in the top berth. I have a state-room trunk which will just slip in under my berth. Where is your luggage?"

Joe looked embarrassed.

"I don't know but you will feel ashamed of me," he said, "but the only extra clothes I have are tied up in this handerchief."

"Well," said he, "you are poorly provided. What have you got inside?"

"A couple of shirts, three collars, two handkerchiefs, and a pair of stockings."

"And this is all you have?"

"Yes."

JOE'S LUCK

"And you are going on a journey of thousands of miles. But never mind," he said, kindly. "I am not much larger than you, and if you need it I can lend you. Now let us go on deck. I think the steamer must be near starting."

They came up just in time to see the steamer swing out of the dock.

"You look happy, Joe," said young Folsom.

"I feel so," said Joe.

"Are you hoping to make your fortune in California?"

"I am hoping to make a living," said Joe.

"Didn't you make a living here at home?"

"A poor living with no prospects ahead. I didn't mind hard work and poor clothes if there had been a prospect of something better by and by."

"Tell me your story. Where were you living and how were you situated?"

Joe told his story, a story already familiar to the reader.

Charles Folsom listened attentively. At the close he said:

"Major Norton didn't appear disposed to pamper you or bring you up in luxury, that's a fact. It would have been hard lines if on account of losing your aunt's legacy you had been compelled to go back to Oakville."

"I wouldn't have gone," said Joe, resolutely.

"Now," said Folsom, "I may as well tell you my story, though as yet it has nothing of romance or adventure in it. I am the son of a New York merchant who is moderately rich. I entered the count-

JOE'S LUCK

ing-room at seventeen, and have remained there ever since, with the exception of four months spent in Europe."

"If you are rich already, why do you go out to California?" asked Joe.

"I am not going to the mines; I am going to prospect a little for the firm. Some day San Francisco will be a large and important commercial city. It may not be in my time, though I think it will be. I am going to see how soon it will pay for our house to establish a branch there."

"I see," said Joe.

Folsom became more and more pleased with his young charge. He saw that he was manly, amiable, and of good principles, with only one great fault—poverty—which he was quite willing to overlook.

They selected seats in the saloon, and were fortunate enough to be assigned to the captain's table. Old travelers know that those who sit at this table are likely to fare better than those who are further removed.

They started from the pier at twelve o'clock. By four o'clock they had made forty miles.

While Folsom was walking the deck with an old friend, whom he had found among the passengers, Joe went on an exploring expedition.

He made his way to that portion of the deck appropriated to the steerage passengers. Among them his eye fell on the man who swindled him. The recognition was mutual.

"You here!" exclaimed the fellow, in amazement.

"Yes," said Joe, "I am here."

JOE'S LUCK

"I thought you said your ticket wasn't good?"

"It wasn't, as you very well know."

"I don't know anything about it. How did you smuggle yourself aboard?"

"I didn't smuggle myself aboard at all. I came on like the rest of the passengers."

"Why haven't I seen you before? I thought I had seen all the steerage passengers."

"I am not a steerage passenger. I am traveling first-class."

"You don't mean it!" ejaculated the fellow, thoroughly astonished. "You told me you hadn't any more money."

"So I did, and that shows that you were the man that sold me the bogus ticket."

"Nothing of the kind," said the other, but he seemed taken aback by Joe's charge. "Well, all I can say is, that you know how to get around. When a man or boy can travel first-class without a cent of money, he'll do."

"I wouldn't have come at all if I had had to swindle a poor boy out of his money," said Joe.

Joe walked off without receiving an answer. He took pains to ascertain the name of the man who had defrauded him. He was entered on the passenger list as Henry Hogan.

"Do you expect to be seasick, Joe?" asked his new guardian.

"I don't know, Mr. Folsom. This is the first time I have ever been at sea."

"I have crossed the Atlantic twice, and been sick each time. I suppose I have a tendency that way."

JOE'S LUCK

"How does it feel?" asked Joe, curiously.

Folsom laughed.

"It cannot be described," he answered. "To be appreciated it must be felt."

"Then I would rather remain ignorant," said Joe.

"You are right. This is a case where ignorance is bliss decidedly."

Twenty-four hours out Folsom's anticipations were realized. He experienced nausea and his head swam.

Returning from a walk on deck, Joe found his guardian lying down in the state-room.

"Is anything the matter, Mr. Folsom?" he asked, anxiously.

"Nothing but what I expected. The demon of the sea has me in his grip."

"Then you are seasick?"

"Yes."

"Can I do anything for you?"

"Nothing at present, Joe. What art can minister to a stomach diseased? I must wait patiently, and it will wear off. Don't you feel any of the symptons?"

"Oh, no—I feel bully," said Joe. "I've got a capital appetite."

"I hope you'll be spared. It would be dismal for both of us to be groaning with seasickness."

"Shall I stay with you?"

"No—go on deck. That is the best way to keep well. My sickness won't last more than a day or two. Then I shall get my sea-legs on, and I shall be all right for the rest of the voyage."

JOE'S LUCK

The young man's expectations were realized. After forty-eight hours he recovered from his temporary indisposition and reappeared on deck.

He found that his young companion had made a number of acquaintances, and had become a general favorite through his frank and pleasant manners, not only with the passengers, but with the officers.

"I think you'll get on, Joe," said he. "You make friends easily."

"I try to do it," said Joe, modestly.

"You are fast getting over your country greenness. Of course, you couldn't help having a share of it, having never lived outside of a small country village."

"I am glad you think so, Mr. Folsom. I suppose I was very green when I first came to the city, and I haven't got over it yet, but in six months I hope to get rid of it wholly."

"It won't take six months at the rate you are advancing."

Day succeeded day, and Joe was not sick at all. He carried a good appetite to every meal, and entered into the pleasures of sea-life with zest. He played shuffle-board on deck, guessed daily the ship's run, was on the alert for distant sails, and managed in one way or another to while away the time cheerfully.

CHAPTER VI

JOE ARRIVES IN SAN FRANCISCO

At the Isthmus they exchanged steamers, crossing the narrow neck of land on the backs of mules. To-day the journey is more rapidly and comfortably made in a railroad car. Of the voyage on the Pacific nothing need be said. The weather was fair, and it was uneventful.

It was a beautiful morning in early September when they came in sight of the Golden Gate, and entering the more placid waters of San Francisco Bay, moored at a short distance from the town.

All the passengers gazed with eager eyes at the port of which they had heard so much—the portal to the Land of Gold.

"What do you think of it, Joe?" asked Charles Folsom.

"I don't know," said Joe, slowly. "Is this really San Francisco?"

"It is really San Francisco."

"It doesn't seem to be much built up yet," said Joe.

In fact, the appearance of the town would hardly suggest the stately capital of to-day, which looks out like a queen on the bay and the ocean, and on either side opens her arms to the Eastern and Western continents. It was a town of tents and one-story cabins, irregularly and picturesquely scattered over the hill-side, with here and there a saw-mill where now stands some of the most prominent buildings of the modern city. For years later there was a large mound of sand where now the stately Palace Hotel covers two and a half acres and proudly challenges the world to show its peer. Where now stand substantial business blocks, a quarter of a century since there appeared only sandy beaches or mud flats, with here and there a wooden pier reaching out into the bay. Only five years before the town contained but seventy-nine buildings—thirty-one frame, twenty-six adobe, and the rest shanties. It had grown largely since then, but even now was only a straggling village, with the air of recent settlement.

"You must remember how new it is. Ten years, nay, five, will work a great change in this straggling village. We shall probably live to see it a city of a hundred thousand inhabitants."

The passengers were eager to land. They were tired of the long voyage and anxious to get on shore. They wanted, as soon as possible, to begin making their fortunes.

"What are your plans, Joe?" asked Charles Folsom.

"I shall accept the first job that offers," said Joe. "I can't afford to remain idle long with my small capital."

"Joe," said the young man, seriously, "let me increase your capital for you."

"Thank you, Mr. Folsom," he said, "you are very kind, but I think it will be better for me to shift on what I have. Then I shall have to go to work at once, and shall get started in my new career."

JOE'S LUCK

"Well, Joe, perhaps you are right. At any rate, I admire your pluck and independent spirit."

There was a motley crowd collected on the pier and on the beach when Joe and his friend landed. Rough, bearded men, in Mexican sombreros and coarse attire—many in shirt-sleeves and with their pantaloons tucked in their boots—watched the new arrivals with interest.

"You needn't feel ashamed of your clothes, Joe," said Folsom, with a smile. "You are better dressed than the majority of those we see."

"They don't look as if they had made their fortunes," he said.

"Don't judge by appearances. In a new country people are careless of appearances. Some of these rough fellows, no doubt have their pockets full of gold."

"Joe, you must dine with me," said Folsom. "Then you may start out for yourself in quest of fortune."

Joe did not know till afterward that the dinners cost five dollars apiece, or he would have been dismayed.

He felt that there was no time for him to lose. He had his fortune to make. Still more important, he had his living to make, and in a place where dollars were held as cheap as dimes in New York or Boston.

So emerging into the street, with his small bundle under his arm, he bent his steps as chance directed.

"I am all ready for a job," he said to himself. "I wonder how soon I shall find one."

Joe knew nothing about the streets or their names. Chance brought him to Clay Street, between what is now Montgomery and Kearny Streets. Outside of a low, wooden building, which appeared to be a restaurant, was a load of wood.

"I wonder if I couldn't get the chance to saw and split that wood?" thought Joe.

It would not do to be bashful. So he went in.

A stout man attired in an apron was waiting on the guests. Joe concluded that this must be the proprietor.

"Sit down, boy," said he, "if you want some dinner."

"I've had my dinner," said Joe. "Don't you want that wood outside sawed and split?"

"Yes. Go ahead."

There was a saw and saw-horse outside. The work was not new to Joe, and he went at it vigorously. No bargain had been made, but Joe knew so little of what would be considered a fair price that in this first instance he chose to leave it to his employer.

While he was thus employed, many persons passed him.

One of them paused and accosted him.

"So you have found work already?" he said.

Looking up, Joe recognized Harry Hogan, the man who had swindled him. He didn't feel inclined to be very social with this man, whom he disliked and despised.

"Yes," said he, coldly.

"Rather strange work for a first-class passenger," said Hogan, with a sneer.

Joe did not choose to be polite to this man, feeling no respect for him.

JOE'S LUCK

Hogan finally moved off.

"I hate that boy," he soliloquized. "He puts on airs for a country boy. So he's getting too proud to talk to me, is he? We'll see, Mr. Joseph Mason. Some time you may be glad enough to ask a favor of me."

Joe kept on till his task was completed. It was about six o'clock, though as Joe had no watch, he had to guess at the hour.

He put on his coat and went into the restaurant.

It was the supper-hour, and again there were guests at the tables.

"I've finished the job," said Joe, in a business-like tone.

The man went to the door and took a look at Joe's work.

"You did it up good," he said. "How much do you want?"

"I don't know," said Joe.

"I will give you some supper and five dollars," said the man.

Joe could hardly believe his ears. Five dollars and a supper for four hours' work! Surely he had come to the Land of Gold in very truth.

"Will that do?"

"Oh, yes," said Joe, candidly.

Joe pocketed the gold-piece which he received with a thrill of exultation. He had never received so much in value for a week's work before. Just then a man paid two dollars for a very plain supper.

"That makes my full pay seven dollars," said Joe to himself. "If I can get steady work, I can get rich very quick," he thought.

JOE'S LUCK

There was one thing, however, that Joe did not take into account. If his earnings were likely to be large, his expenses would be large too. So he might receive a good deal of money and not lay up a cent.

"Shall you have any more work to do?" asked Joe, when he had finished his supper.

"Not just now," answered the man. "You can look around in a week. Maybe I will have some then."

Joe walked about the streets with his money in his pocket, feeling in very good spirits.

CHAPTER VII

JOE'S SECOND DAY

Before going to the Leidesdorff House to call upon his friend Folsom, Joe thought he would try to make arrangements for the night. He must have some place to sleep in, and as cheap as possible.

He came to the St. Francis Hotel, on the corner of Dupont and Clay Streets.

A man came out from a room which served as the office.

"Can I get lodging here?" asked Joe.

"Yes."

"How much do you charge?"

"Three dollars."

"I can't afford it," he said.

"All right," said the man.

Continuing his wanderings, Joe came to a tent, which seemed to be a hotel in its way, for it had "LODGINGS" inscribed on the canvas in front.

"What do you charge for lodgings?" Joe inquired of a man who was sitting on the ground in front.

"A dollar," was the reply.

Looking in, Joe saw that the accommodations were of the plainest. Thin pallets were spread about without pillows. Joe was not used to luxury, but to sleep here would be roughing it even for him. But he was prepared to rough it, and concluded that he might as well pass the night here.

"All right!" said he. "I'll be round by and by."

Joe went on to the Leidesdorff Hotel, and was cordially received by Mr. Folsom.

"How much have you earned to-day, Joe?"

"Five dollars and my supper."

"That's good. Is the job finished?"

"Yes, sir."

"And you have nothing else in view for to-morrow, Joe?"

"No, sir; but I guess I shall run across a job."

"I am thinking of making a trip to the mines," continued Folsom. "Very likely I shall start to-morrow. Do you want to go with me?"

"I expect to go to the mines some time," said Joe, "but I think I had better remain a while in San Francisco, and try to lay by a little money. You know I am in debt."

"There is no hurry about it, Joe. Don't let that trouble you."

"I'd like to get it off my mind, Mr. Folsom."

About nine o'clock Joe left the hotel and sought

the tent where he proposed to pass the night. He was required to pay in advance, and willingly did so.

Joe woke up at seven o'clock the next morning. Though his bed was hard he slept well, for he was fatigued. He stretched himself and sat up on his pallet.

He got up and went out in search of breakfast. He thought of the place where he took supper the night before, but was deterred from going there by the high prices.

"I suppose I shall have to pay a dollar for my breakfast," he thought, "but I can't afford to pay two. My capital is reduced to five dollars and I may not be able to get anything to do to-day."

He finally succeeded in finding a humble place where for a dollar he obtained a cup of coffee, a plate of cold meat, and as much bread as he could eat.

After breakfast Joe walked about the streets hoping that something would turn up. But his luck did not seem to be so good as the day before. Hour after hour passed and no chance offered itself.

About four o'clock Joe went into a restaurant and got some dinner. He was hungry, having eaten nothing since breakfast, and having spent the intervening time in walking about the town. In spite of his wish to be economical, his dinner bill amounted to a dollar and a half, and now his cash in hand was reduced to two dollars and a half.

Joe began to feel uneasy.

"This won't do," he said to himself. "At this rate

JOE'S LUCK

I shall soon be penniless. I must get something or other to do."

In the evening he strolled down Montgomery Street to Telegraph Hill. It was not a very choice locality, the only buildings being shabby little dens, frequented by a class of social outlaws who kept concealed during the day but came out at night—a class to which the outrages upon the person frequent at this time were rightly attributed.

If Joe had understood better the character of this neighborhood, he would not have ventured there in the evening.

Joe was stumbling along the uneven path, when all at once he found himself confronted by a tall fellow wearing a slouched hat. The man paused in front of him, but did not say a word. Finding that he was not disposed to move aside, Joe stepped aside himself. He did not as yet suspect the fellow's purpose. He understood it, however, when a heavy hand was laid on his shoulder.

"Quick, boy, your money!" said the ruffian.

Having but two dollars and a half, Joe naturally felt reluctant to part with it, and this gave him the courage to object.

"I've got none to spare," he said.

Joe felt himself seized and carried into a den close by, which was frequented by thieves and desperate characters.

"You'd better hand over what you've got, young 'un."

Joe resigned himself to the loss of his money, inconvenient as it might prove to him. His only thought now was to get away. He drew out the balance of his money and held it out to his captor.

"There is my money," he said.

"Is that all you've got?" demanded the thief.

"You may go," said his captor as he opened the door of the den; "and don't come around here again unless you've got money with you."

"I don't think I shall," said Joe.

The door was closed, and he found himself in the darkness, a little uncertain at first as to where he should direct his steps.

It is rather a singular circumstance that now, when Joe found himself penniless, he really felt less anxious than a few minutes before, when he had at least money enough to pay for lodging and breakfast. It might have been on the principle that the darkest hour is just before day. Having lost everything, any turn of fortune must be for the better.

"Something has got to turn up pretty quick," thought Joe. "It's just as well I didn't get a job to-day. I should only have had more money to lose."

He had not walked a hundred feet when his attention was called to the figure of a gentleman walking some rods in front of him. He saw it but indistinctly, and would not have given it a second thought, had he not seen that the person, whoever he might be, was stealthily followed by a man who in general appearance resembled the rascal who had robbed him of his money. The pursuer carried in his hand a canvas bag filled with sand.

Though Joe didn't comprehend the use of the sandbag, his own recent experience and the stealthy

JOE'S LUCK

movement of the man behind convinced him that mischief was intended. He felt a chivalrous desire to rescue the unsuspecting stranger from the peril that menaced him. There was little time to think or resolve. The time demanded instant action.

Joe, too, imitating the stealthy motion of the pursuer, swiftly gained upon him, overtaking him just as he had the sandbag poised aloft, ready to be brought down upon the head of the traveler.

With a cry, Joe, exerting all his strength, rushed upon the would-be assassin, causing him to stumble and fall, while the gentleman in front turned round in amazement.

Joe sprung to his side.

"Have you a pistol?" he said quickly.

Scarcely knowing what he did, the gentleman drew out a pistol and put it in Joe's hand. Joe cocked it, and stood facing the ruffian.

He was only just in time.

The desperado was on his feet, fury in his looks and a curse upon his lips. He swung the sand-bag aloft.

"Curse you!" he said. "I'll make you pay for this."

"One step forward," said Joe, in a clear, distinct voice which betrayed not a particle of fear, "and I will put a bullet through your brain."

The assassin stepped back. He was a coward who attacked from behind. He looked in the boy's resolute face, and he saw he was in earnest.

"Now turn round and leave us."

"Will you promise not to shoot?" said the villain.

"Yes, if you go off quietly."

JOE'S LUCK

The order was obeyed, but not very willingly.

When the highwayman had moved far enough off Joe said:

"Now, sir, we'd better be moving, and pretty quickly, or the fellow may return with some of his friends and overpower us. Where are you stopping?"

"At the Waverly House."

"That is nearby. We will go there at once."

They soon reached the hotel, a large wooden building on the north side of Pacific Street, between Montgomery and Kearny.

Joe was about to bid his acquaintance good-night, but the latter detained him.

"Come in, my boy," he said heartily. "You have done me a great service to-night. I must know more of you."

CHAPTER VIII

JOE'S NEW FRIEND

"Come up to my room," said the stranger.

"You were a friend in need, and they say a friend in need is a friend indeed. It is only fair that I should be a friend to you. It's a poor rule that doesn't work both ways."

Joe was favorably impressed with the speaker's appearance. He was a man of middle height, rather stout, with a florid complexion and an open, friendly face. It struck Joe that he would be a good friend to have.

JOE'S LUCK

"Thank you, sir," he said. "I need a friend, and shall be glad of your friendship."

"Then," said he, "here's my hand. Take it, and let us ratify our friendship."

Joe took the proffered hand and shook it cordially.

"My name is George Morgan," said the stranger. "I came from Philadelphia. Now we know each other. Where are you staying?"

Joe's face flushed, and he looked embarrassed.

"Just before I came up with you," he answered thinking frankness best, "I was robbed of two dollars and a half, all the money I had in this world. I shall have to stop in the streets to-night."

"Not if I know it," said Morgan, emphatically. "This bed isn't very large, but you are welcome to a share of it. To-morrow we will form our plans."

"Shan't I inconvenience you, sir?" asked Joe.

"Not a bit," answered Morgan, heartily. "I shall be glad of your company."

"Then I will stay, sir, and thank you. After the adventure I have had to-night, I shouldn't enjoy being out in the streets."

"Tell me how you came to be robbed."

Joe gave an account of the robbery to which his new friend listened with attention.

"Evidently," he said, "the street we were in is not a very safe one. We may as well avoid it in future. I am tired I will go to bed, and you can follow when you feel inclined."

"I will go now, sir. I have been walking the streets all day in search of work, and though I found none, I am tired all the same."

JOE'S LUCK

In half an hour both Joe and his new friend were fast asleep.

They woke up at seven o'clock.

"How did you rest, Joe?" asked George Morgan.

"Very well, sir."

"Do you feel ready for breakfast? You are going to breakfast with me."

"You are very kind, Mr. Morgan, but I wish you had some work for me to do so that I could pay you."

"That may come after awhile. Remember you have done me a great service which fifty breakfasts couldn't pay for."

They took breakfast in the hotel and then walked out.

They were walking on Kearny Street, near California Street, when Joe's attention was drawn to a sign:

THIS RESTAURANT FOR SALE.

It was a one-story building, of small dimensions, not fashionable nor elegant in its appointments, but there wasn't much style in San Francisco at that time. People didn't come out for that.

"Would you like to buy out the restaurant?" asked Morgan.

"I don't feel like buying anything out with empty pockets," said Joe.

"Let us go in."

The proprietor of the restaurant was a sandy-haired man, of middle age.

"Why do you wish to sell out?" asked Morgan.

"I want to go to the mines. I need an out-of-door life, and want a change."

"Does this business pay?"

"Sometimes I have made seventy-five dollars profit in a day."

"That's good. How much do you ask for the business?"

"I'll take five hundred dollars cash."

"Have you a reliable cook?"

"Yes. He knows his business."

"Will he stay?"

"For the present. If you want a profitable business you will do well to buy."

"I don't want it for myself. I want it for this young man."

"For this boy?" asked the restaurant-keeper surprised.

Joe looked equally surprised.

Do you think you can keep a hotel, Joe?" asked Morgan.

"I can try," said Joe, promptly.

"Come in, gentlemen," said the restaurant-keeper. "We can talk best inside."

The room was small, holding but six tables. In the rear was the kitchen.

"Let me see your scale of prices," said Morgan.

It was shown him.

"I could breakfast cheaper at Delmonico's," he said.

"And better," said the proprietor of the restaurant, "but I find people here willing to pay big prices, and as long as that's the case, I should be a fool to reduce them. Yes, there's a splendid profit to be made in the business. I ought to charge a thousand dollars instead of five hundred."

"Why don't you?" asked Morgan, bluntly.

"Because I couldn't get it. Most men when they come out here are not content to settle down in the town. They won't be satisfied till they get to the mines."

"That seems to be the case with you, too."

"It isn't that altogether. My lungs are weak, and confinement isn't good for me. Besides, the doctors say the climate in the interior is better for pulmonary affections."

"What rent do you have to pay?"

"A small ground-rent. I put up this building myself."

"How soon can you give possession?"

"Right off."

"Will you stay here three days to initiate my young friend into the mysteries of the business?"

"Oh, yes, I'll do that willingly."

"Then I will buy you out."

In five minutes the business was settled.

"Joe," said Morgan, "let me congratulate you. You are now one of the business men of San Francisco."

"It seems like a dream to me, Mr. Morgan," said Joe. "This morning when I waked up I wasn't worth a cent."

"And now you own five hundred dollars."

"That wasn't exactly the way I thought of it, sir, but are you not afraid to trust me to that amount?"

"No, I am not, Joe," said Morgan, seriously. "I

think you are a boy of energy and integrity. I don't see why you shouldn't succeed."

"Suppose I shouldn't?"

"I shall not trouble myself about the loss. In all probability you saved my life last evening. That is worth to me many times what I've invested for you."

"I want to give you my note for the money."

"I agree with you. We may as well put it on a business basis."

Papers were drawn out, and Joe found himself proprietor of the restaurant.

"Do you live here, Mr. Brock?" asked Joe.

"Yes; I have a bed which I lay in the corner of the restaurant. Thus I avoid the expense of a room outside, and am on hand early for business."

"I'll do the same," said Joe, promptly.

In two days Joe, who was naturally quick, and whose natural shrewdness was sharpened by his personal interest, mastered the details of the business, and felt that he could manage alone.

"Mr. Brock," said he, "you promised to stay with me three days, but I won't insist upon the third day. I think I can get along well without you."

"If you can, I shall be glad to leave you at once."

So on the morning of the third day Joe found himself alone.

At the end of the first week he made a careful estimate of his expenses and receipts, and found to his astonishment that he had cleared two hundred dollars.

"Two hundred dollars in one week!" he said to himself. "What would Oscar say to that? It seems like a fairy tale."

JOE'S LUCK

Joe did not forget that he was five hundred dollars in debt. He went to George Morgan, who had bought out for himself a gentlemen's furnishing store, and said:

"Mr. Morgan, I want to pay up a part of that debt."

"So soon, Joe? How much do you want to pay?"

"A hundred and fifty dollars."

"Very well. I will receive the money. You do well to wipe out your debts as soon as possible."

Without going too much into detail, it may be stated that at the end of a month Joe was out of debt and had three hundred dollars over. He called on the owner of the land to pay the monthly ground-rent.

"Why don't you buy the land, and get rid of the rent?"

"Do you want to sell?" asked Joe.

"Yes; I am about to return to the East."

"What do you ask?"

"I own two adjoining lots. You may have them all for a thousand dollars."

"Will you give me time?"

"I can't I want to return at once, and I must have the cash."

"I will take three hours to consider," he said.

He went to George Morgan and broached his business.

"Mr. Morgan," he said, "will you lend me seven hundred dollars?"

"Are you getting into pecuniary difficulties, Joe?"

"No, sir; but I want to buy some real estate."

JOE'S LUCK

"Explain yourself."

Joe did so.

"It is the best thing you can do," said Morgan. "I will lend you the money."

"I hope to repay it inside of two months," said Joe.

"I think you will, judging from what you have done already."

In two hours Joe had paid over the entire amount, for it will be remembered that he had three hundred dollars of his own, and was owner of three city lots.

"How shall I make my restaurant more attractive?" thought Joe.

He decided first that he would buy good articles and insist upon as much neatness as possible about the tables.

Soon Joe's dining-room acquired a reputation and the patronage increased.

One day about this time, as he was at the desk where he received money from his patrons as they went out, his attention was drawn to a rough fellow having the appearance of a tramp entering at the door. The man's face seemed familiar to him, and it flashed upon him that it was Henry Hogan, who had defrauded him in New York.

The recognition was mutual.

"You here?" he exclaimed in surprise.

"So it seems," said Joe.

"Is it a good place?"

"I like it."

"Who's your boss?"

"Myself."

JOE'S LUCK

"You don't mean to say this is your own place?"
"Yes, I do."
"Well, I'll be blowed!" ejaculated Hogan.

CHAPTER IX

MR. HOGAN'S PROPOSAL

Joe enjoyed Hogan's amazement. He felt rather proud of his rapid progress. It was not four months since, a poor country boy, he had come up to New York and fallen a prey to a designing sharper. Now, on the other side of the continent, he was a master of a business and owner of real estate.

"How have you made out?" asked Joe, of his visitor.

"I've had hard luck," grumbled Hogan. "I went to the mines but I wasn't lucky."

"Was that the case with other miners?" asked Joe.

"No," said Hogan. "Other men around me were lucky, but I wasn't. You've got on well. You're lucky."

"Yes, I have no reason to complain. But I wasn't lucky all the time. I was robbed of every cent of money, when I met a good friend who bought this business for me."

"Does it pay?" asked the other, eagerly.

"Yes, it pays," said Joe, cautiously.

"Will you trust me for my supper?"

"Yes," said Joe, promptly. "Sit down at that table."

JOE'S LUCK

The man had treated him badly, but things had turned out favorably for Joe, and he would not let Hogan suffer from hunger if he could relieve him.

Hogan needed no second invitation.

"You've got a good cook," said Hogan, when he had finished.

"Yes," answered Joe. "I think so."

"Are you alone? Have you no partner?"

"No."

"You could do better with one. Suppose you take me into the business with you."

"I don't want any partner, Mr. Hogan," he said, "and I may as well tell you I don't think I should care to be associated with you if I did."

"Look here, young one, you put on too many airs just because you're keepin' a one-horse restaurant," said Hogan, angrily.

"If it's a one-horse restaurant, why do you want to become my partner?" retorted Joe, coolly.

"Because I'm hard up—I haven't got a cent."

"I'm sorry for you, but a man needn't be in that condition long here."

"Where do you sleep?" asked Hogan suddenly.

"Here. I put a bed on the floor in one corner, and so am on hand in the morning."

"I say," continued Hogan insinuatingly, "won't you let me stay here to-night?"

"I'd rather not, Mr. Hogan."

"I haven't a cent to pay for a lodging. If you don't take me in, I shall have to stay in the street all night."

"You've slept out at the mines, haven't you?"

JOE'S LUCK

"You're hard on a poor man," whined Hogan. "It wouldn't cost you anything to let me sleep here."

"No, it wouldn't," said Joe, "but I prefer to choose my own company at night."

"You haven't any feeling for an unlucky man."

"I have given you your supper, and not stinted you in any way. What you ate would cost two dollars at my regular prices. I wasn't called to do it, for you never did me any service, and you are owing me to-day fifty dollars, which you cheated me out of when I was a poor boy. I won't let you lodge here, but I will give you a breakfast in the morning, if you choose to come around. Then you will be strengthened for a day's work and can see what you can find to do."

Hogan saw that Joe was in earnest, and walked out of the restaurant without a word.

When Joe was about to close his doors for the night, his attention was drawn to a man who was sitting down on the ground, a few feet distant, with his head buried between his two hands, in an attitude expressive of despondency.

"Is anything the matter with you, sir?" he asked. "Don't you feel well?"

The man addressed raised his head. He was a stout, strongly built man, roughly dressed, but had a look which inspired confidence.

"I may as well tell you, boy," he answered, "though you can't help me. I've been a cursed fool, that's what's the matter."

"If you don't mind telling me," said Joe, gently, "perhaps I can be of service to you."

JOE'S LUCK

The man shook his head.

"I don't think you can," he said, "but I'll tell you for all that. Yesterday I came up from the mines with two thousand dollars. I was about a year getting it together, and to me it was a fortune. I'm a shoemaker by occupation, and lived in a town in Massachussetts, where I have a wife and two children. I left them a year ago to go to the mines. I did well, and the money I told you about would have made us all comfortable if I could only have got it home."

"Were you robbed of it?" asked Joe, remembering his own experience.

"Yes, I was robbed of it, but not in the way you are thinking of. A wily scoundrel induced me to enter a gambling-den, the Bella Union they called it. I wouldn't play at first, but soon the fascination seized me. I saw a man win a hundred dollars, and I thought I could do the same, so I began and won a little. Then I lost, and played on to get my money back. In just an hour I was cleaned out of all I had. Now I am penniless and my poor family will suffer for my folly."

He buried his face in his hands once more, and strong man as he was, he wept aloud.

"Have you had any supper, sir?" asked Joe, compassionately.

"No, but I have no appetite."

"Have you any place to sleep?"

"No."

"Then I can offer you a supper and a night's lodging. Don't be discouraged. In the morn-

JOE'S LUCK

ing we can talk the matter over and see what can be done."

The stranger rose and laid his hand on Joe's arm. "I don't know how it is," he said, "but your words give me courage. I believe you have saved my life. I have a revolver left, and I had a mind to blow my brains out."

"Would that have helped you or your family?"

"No, boy. I was a fool to think of it. I'll accept your offer, and to-morrow I'll see what I can do. You're the best friend I've met since I left home."

Joe brought out some cold meat and bread and butter, and set it before his guest.

"The fire's gone out," he said, "or I would give you some tea. Here's a glass of milk, if you like it."

"Thank you, boy," said his visitor. "Milk is good enough for anybody. One thing I can say, I've steered clear of liquor. A brother of mine was intemperate, and that was a warning to me. I took credit to myself for being a steady-going man compared with many of my acquaintances out at the mines. But it don't do to boast. I've done worse, perhaps. I've gambled away the provision I had made for my poor family."

"Don't take it too hard," said Joe, in a tone of sympathy. "You know how it is out here. Down to-day and up to-morrow."

"It'll take me a long time to get up to where I was," said the other, "but it's my fault, and I must make the best of it."

"I didn't think I could eat anything," said the miner, laying down his knife and fork, twenty min-

JOE'S LUCK

utes later, "but I have made a hearty supper, thanks to your kindness. Things look a little brighter to me now. I've had a hard pull-back, but all is not lost. I've got to stay here a year or two longer instead of going back by the next steamer; but I must make up my mind to that. What is your name, boy?"

"Joe Mason."

"You've been kind to me, and I won't forget it. It doesn't seem likely I can return the favor, but I'll do it if ever I can. Good-night to you."

"Where are you going?" asked Joe, surprised, as the miner walked to the door.

"Out into the street."

"But where do you mean to pass the night?"

"Where a man without money must—in the street."

"But you mustn't do that."

"I shan't mind it. I've slept out at the mines many a night."

"But won't you find it more comfortable here?"

"Yes, but I don't want to intrude. You've given me a good supper, and that is all I can expect."

"You are welcome to lodge here with me," he said. "It will cost me nothing, and will be more comfortable for you."

"You don't know me, Joe," said the miner. "How do you know but I may get up in the night and rob you?"

"You could, but I don't think you will," said Joe. "I am not at all afraid of it. You look like an honest man."

The miner looked gratified.

JOE'S LUCK

"You shan't repent your confidence, Joe," he said. "I'd rather starve than rob a good friend like you. But you mustn't trust everybody."

"I don't," said Joe. "I refused a man to-night—a man named Hogan."

"Hogan?"

"Yes."

"What does he look like?"

Joe described him.

"It's the very man," said the miner.

"Do you know him, then?"

"Yes; he was out at our diggings. Nobody liked him or trusted him. He was too lazy to work, but just loafed around, complaining of his luck. One night I caught him in my tent just going to rob me. I warned him to leave the camp next day or I'd report him, and the boys would have strung him up. That's the way they treat thieves out there."

"It doesn't surprise me to hear it," said Joe. "He robbed me of fifty dollars in New York."

"He did? How was that?"

Joe told the story.

"The mean skunk!" ejaculated Watson—for this Joe found to be the miner's name. "It's mean enough to rob a man, but to cheat a poor boy out of all he has is a good deal meaner. And yet you gave him supper?"

"Yes. The man was hungry; I pitied him."

"You're a better Christian than I am. I'd have let him go hungry."

Both Joe and the miner were weary, and they soon retired, but not to uninterrupted slumber.

JOE'S LUCK

About mid-night they were disturbed, as the next chapter will show.

CHAPTER X

HOGAN MEETS A CONGENIAL SPIRIT

When Hogan left Joe's presence he was far from feeling as grateful as he ought for the kindness with which our hero had treated him.

Out in the street he paused a minute, undecided where to go. He had no money, as he had truly said, or he would have been tempted to go to a gambling-house and risk it on a chance of making more.

The more Hogan thought of this the more indignant he became.

"I say it's a cursed shame!" he muttered, "I never did have any luck, that's a fact. Just see how luck comes to some. With only a dollar or two in his pocket this Joe got trusted for a first-class passage out here, while I had to come in the steerage. Then again he meets some fool who sets him up in business. Nobody ever offered to set me up in business!" continued Hogan, feeling aggrieved at Fortune for her partiality. "Nobody even offered to give me a start in life. I have to work hard, and that's all the good it does."

Then Hogan drifted off into calculations of how much money Joe was making by his business. He knew the prices charged for meals, and that they afforded a large margin of profit.

JOE'S LUCK

"The boy must be making his fortune," he said to himself. "Why he can't help from clearing from one to two hundred dollars a week—perhaps more. It's a money making business, there's no doubt of it. Why couldn't he take me in as partner? That would set me on my legs again and in time I'd be rich. I'd make him sell out and get the whole thing after awhile."

Sauntering slowly along Hogan had reached the corner of Pacific Street, then a dark and suspicious locality in the immediate neighborhood of a number of low public-houses of bad reputation. The night was dark, for there was no moon.

Suddenly he felt himself seized in a tight grip, while a low, stern voice in his ear demanded:

"Your money, and be quick about it!"

"You've got the wrong man!" he chuckled.

"Stop your fooling and hand over your money quickly."

"My dear friend," said Hogan, "if you can find any money about me it's more than I can do myself."

"Are you on the square?" demanded the other.

"Look at me and see."

The highwayman took him at his word. Lighting a match he surveyed his captive.

"You don't look wealthy, that's a fact," he admitted. "Where are you going?"

"I don't know. I haven't got any money nor any place to sleep."

"Then you'd better be leaving this place or another mistake may be made."

"Stop," said Hogan, with a sudden thought.

JOE'S LUCK

"Though I haven't any money, I can tell you where we can both find some."

"Do you mean it?"

"Yes."

"Come in here, then, and come to business."

He led Hogan into a low shanty on Pacific Street, and bidding him be seated on a broken settee, waited for particulars.

Though Hogan was a scamp in the superlative degree, the burly ruffian who seated himself by his side looked the character much better. He was not a man to beat about the bush. As he expressed it, he wanted to come to business at once.

"What's your game, pard?" he demanded. "Out with it."

Hogan's plan, as the reader has already surmised, was to break into Joe's restaurant and seize whatever money he might be found to have on the premises. He recommended it earnestly for two reasons. First, a share of the money would be welcome, and secondly, he would be gratified to revenge himself upon the boy whom he disliked because he had injured him.

Jack Rafferty listened in silence.

"I don't know about it," he said. "There's a risk."

"I don't see any risk. We two ought to be a match for a boy."

"Of course we are. If we wasn't I'd go hang myself up for a milksop. Are you sure there's no one else with him?"

"Not a soul."

JOE'S LUCK

"That's well so far, but we might be seen from the outside."

"We can keep watch."

"Do you think the boy's got much money about him?"

"Yes—he's making money hand over fist. He's one of those mean chaps that never spend a cent, but lay it all by."

So Hogan expressed his contempt for Joe's frugality.

"All the better for us. How much might there be now, do you think?"

"Five hundred dollars, likely."

"That's worth risking something for," said Jack.

"We'll share alike?" inquired Hogan, anxiously.

"Depends on how much you help about gettin' the money," said Jack, carelessly.

Hogan, who was not very courageous, did not dare push the matter, though he would have liked a more definite assurance. However, he had another motive besides the love of money, and was glad to have the co-operation of Rafferty, though secretly afraid of his ruffianly accomplice.

It was agreed to wait till midnight. Till then both men threw themselves down and slept.

As the clock indicated midnight, Rafferty shook Hogan roughly.

The latter sat up and gazed in terrified bewilderment at Jack, who was leaning over him, forgetting for the moment the compact into which he had entered.

"What do you want?" he ejaculated.

"It's time we were about our business," growled Jack. "It's struck twelve."

"All right," responded Hogan, who began to feel nervous now that the crisis was at hand.

"Don't sit rubbing your eyes, man, but get up."

"Haven't you got a drop of something to brace me up?" asked Hogan, nervously.

"What are you scared of, pard?" asked Rafferty, contemptuously.

"Nothing," answered Hogan, "but I feel dry."

"All right. A drop of something will warm us both up."

Jack went behind the counter, and selecting a bottle of whisky, poured out a stiff glassful apiece.

"Drink it, pard," he said.

Hogan did so, nothing loath.

"That's the right sort," he said, smacking his lips. "It's warming to the stomach."

So it was, and a frequent indulgence in the vile liquid would probably have burned his stomach and unfitted it for service. But the momentary effect was stimulating, and inspired Hogan with a kind of Dutch courage, which raised him in the opinion of his burly confederate.

"Push ahead, pard," said he. "I'm on hand."

"That's the way to talk," said Rafferty, approvingly.

Through the dark streets, unlighted and murky, the two confederates made their stealthy way, and in five minutes stood in front of Joe's restaurant.

Everything looked favorable for their plans. Of

course, the restaurant was perfectly dark, and the street was quite deserted.

"How shall we get in?" asked Hogan of his more experienced accomplice.

"No trouble—through the winder."

Rafferty had served an apprenticeship at the burglar's trade, and was not long in opening the front window. He had no light, and could not see that Joe had a companion. If he had discovered this he would have been more cautious.

"Go in and get the money," said he to Hogan.

He thought it possible that Hogan might object, but the latter had a reason for consenting. He thought he might obtain for himself the lion's share of the plunder, while as to risk, there would be no one but Joe to cope with, and Hogan knew that in physical strength he must be more than a match for a boy of sixteen.

"All right!" said Hogan. "You stay at the window and give the alarm if we are seen."

Rafferty was prompted by a suspicion of Hogan's good faith in the proposal he made to him. His ready compliance lulled this suspicion, and led him to reflect that perhaps he could do the work better himself.

"No," said he, "I'll go in, and you keep watch at the winder."

Rafferty clambered into the room, making as little noise as possible. He stood still a moment to accustom his eyes to the darkness. His plan was to discover where Joe lay, wake him up, and force him, by threats of instant death as the penalty for non-

JOE'S LUCK

compliance, to deliver up all the money he had in the restaurant.

Now, it happened that Joe and his guest slept in opposite corners of the room. Rafferty discovered Joe, but was entirely ignorant of the presence of another person in the apartment.

"Who is it?" he muttered drowsily.

"Never mind who it is," growled Jack in his ear. "It's a man that'll kill you if you don't give up all the money you've got about you."

Joe was fully awake now and realized the situation. He felt thankful that he was not alone, and it instantly flashed upon him that Watson had a revolver. But Watson was asleep. To obtain time to form a plan, he parleyed a little.

"You want my money?" he asked, appearing to be confused.

"Yes, and at once. Refuse, and I will kill you."

I won't pretend to deny that Joe's heart beat a little quicker than its wont. He was thinking busily. How could he attract Watson's attention?"

"It's pretty hard, but I suppose I must," he answered.

"That's the way to talk."

"Let me up, and I'll get it."

Joe spoke so naturally that Rafferty suspected nothing. He permitted our hero to rise, supposing that he was going for the money he demanded.

Joe knew exactly where Watson lay, and went over to him. He knelt down and drew out the revolver from beneath his head, at the same time pushing him in the hope of arousing him. The push was effectual. Watson was a man whose experience at the mines had taught him to rouse at once. He just heard Joe say:

"Hush!"

"What are you so long about?" demanded Rafferty.

"I've got a revolver," said Joe, unexpectedly, "and if you don't leave the room I'll fire."

With an oath, Rafferty, who was no coward, sprung upon Joe, and it would have gone hard with him but for Watson. The latter was now broad awake. He seized Rafferty by the collar, and dashing him backward upon the floor, threw himself upon him.

"Two can play at that game," said he. "Light the candle, Joe."

"Help, pard!" called Rafferty.

But Hogan, on whom he called, suspecting how matters stood, was in full flight.

The candle was lighted, and in the struggling ruffian Joe recognized the man who, three months before, had robbed him of his little all.

CHAPTER XI

NOT WHOLLY BLACK

"I know this man, Mr. Watson," said Joe.

"Who is he?"

"He is the same man who robbed me of my money one night about three months ago—the one I told you of."

JOE'S LUCK

For the first time Rafferty recognized Joe.

"There wasn't enough to make a fuss about," he said.

"It was all I had."

"Let me up!" said Rafferty, renewing his struggles.

"Joe, have you got a rope?" asked Watson.

"Yes."

"Bring it here, then. I can't hold this man all night."

"What are you going to do with me?"

"Tie you hand and foot till to-morrow morning, and then deliver you over to the authorities."

"No, you won't."

He made a renewed struggle, but Watson was a man with muscles of iron, and the attempt was unsuccessful.

It was not without considerable difficulty, however, that the midnight intruder was secured. When, at length, he was bound hand and foot, Watson withdrew to a little distance. Joe and he looked at Rafferty, and each felt that he had seldom seen a more brutal face.

"Well," growled Rafferty, "I hope you are satisfied."

"Not yet," returned Watson. "When you are delivered into the hands of the authorities we shall be satisfied."

"Oh, for an hour's freedom!" muttered Jack Rafferty.

"What use would you make of it?" asked Watson.

"I'd kill the man that led me into this trap."

JOE'S LUCK

Watson and Joe were surprised.

"Was there such a man? Didn't you come here alone?"

"No—there was a man got me to come. Curse him, he told me I would find only the boy here."

"What has become of him?"

"He ran away, I reckon, instead of standing by me."

"Where was he?"

"At the winder."

"Could it have been Hogan?" thought Joe.

"I think I know the man," said our hero. "I'll describe the man I mean, and you can tell me if it was he."

He described Hogan as well as he could.

"That's the man," said Rafferty. "I wouldn't peach if he hadn't served me such a mean trick. What's his name?"

"His name is Hogan. He came over on the same steamer with me, after robbing me of fifty dollars in New York. He has been at the mines, but didn't make out well. This very afternoon I gave him supper—all he could eat—and charged him nothing for it. He repays me by planning a robbery."

"I'm a scamp myself, but I'll be blowed if I'd turn on a man that fed me when I was hungry."

The tones were gruff, but the man was evidently sincere.

"You're better than you look," said Watson.

Jack Rafferty laughed shortly.

"I ain't used to compliments," he said, "and I expect I'm bad enough, but I ain't all bad. I won't turn

JOE'S LUCK

on my pal unless he does it first, and I ain't mean enough to rob the man that's done me a good turn."

"No, you ain't all bad," said Watson. "It's a pity you won't make up your mind to earn an honest living."

"Too late for that, I reckon. What do you think they'll do with me?"

In those days punishments were summary and severe. Watson knew it and Joe had seen something of it. Our hero began to feel compassion for the foiled burglar. He whispered in Watson's ear. Watson hesitated, but finally yielded.

"Stranger," said he, "the boy wants me to let you go."

"Does he?" inquired Rafferty, in surprise.

"Yes. He is afraid it will go hard with you if we give you up."

"Likely it will," muttered Rafferty, watching Watson's face eagerly to see whether he favored Joe's proposal.

"Suppose we let you go—will you promise not to make another attempt upon this place?"

"What do you take me for? I'm not such a mean cuss as that."

"One thing more—you won't kill this man that brought you here?"

"If I knowed it wasn't a trap he led me into. He told me there was only the boy."

"He thought so. I don't belong here. The boy let me sleep here out of kindness. Hogan knew nothing of this. I didn't come till after he had left."

"That's different," said Rafferty; "but he shouldn't have gone back on me."

"He is a coward, probably."

"I guess you're right," said Rafferty, contemptuously.

"You promise then?"

"Yes."

"Then we'll let you go."

Watson unloosed the bonds that confined the prisoner. Rafferty raised himself to his full height and stretched his limbs.

"There, I feel better," he said. "You tied the rope pretty tight."

"I found it necessary," said Watson, laughing. "Now, Joe, if you will open the door this gentleman will pass out."

Rafferty turned to Joe as he was about to leave the restaurant.

"Boy," said he, "I won't forget this. I ain't much of a friend to boast of, but I'm your friend. You've saved me from prison and worse, it's likely, and if you need help any time send for me. If I had that money I took from you I'd pay it back."

"I don't need it," said Joe. "I've been lucky and am doing well. I hope you'll make up your mind to turn over a new leaf. If you do, and are ever hard up for a meal, come to me, and you shall have it without money and without price."

"Thank you, boy," said Rafferty. "I'll remember it."

He strode out of the restaurant and disappeared in the darkness.

JOE'S LUCK

"Human nature's a curious thing, Joe," said Watson. "Who would have expected to find any redeeming quality in such a man as that?"

"I would sooner trust him than Hogan."

"So would I. Hogan is a mean scoundrel, who is not so much of a ruffian as this man only because he is too much of a coward to be."

"I am glad we let him go," said Joe.

"I am not sure whether it was best. He won't trouble you any more."

"I wish I felt as sure about Hogan," said Joe.

"Hogan is a coward. I advise you to keep a revolver constantly on hand. He won't dare to break in by himself."

* * * * * * *

The next morning after breakfast Watson prepared to go out in search of work.

"I must begin at the bottom of the ladder once more," he said to Joe. "It's my own fault and I won't complain. But what a fool I have been! I might have gone home by the next steamer if I hadn't gambled away all my hard earnings."

"What sort of work shall you try to get?"

"Anything—I have no right to be particular. Anything that will pay my expenses and give me a chance to lay something by for my family at home."

"Mr. Watson," said Joe, suddenly, "I've been thinking of something that may suit you. Since I came to San Francisco I have never gone outside. I would like to go to the mines."

"You wouldn't make as much as you do here."

"Perhaps not, but I have laid by some money and

JOE'S LUCK

I would like to see something of the country. Will you carry on the restaurant for me for three months if I give you your board and half of the profits?"

"Will I? I should think myself very lucky to get the chance."

"Then you shall have the chance."

"How do you know that I can be trusted?" asked Watson.

"I haven't known you long," said Joe, "but I feel confidence in your honesty."

"I don't think you'll repent your confidence. When do you want to go?"

"I'll stay here a few days till you get used to the business, then I will start."

"I was lucky to fall in with you," said Watson "I didn't want to go back to the mines and tell the boys what a fool I have been. I begin to think there's a chance for me yet."

CHAPTER XII

MR. BICKFORD OF PUMPKIN HOLLOW

It may be thought that Joe was rash in deciding to leave his business in the hands of a man whose acquaintance he had made but twelve hours previous. But in the early history of California friendships ripened fast.

Joe went round to his friend, Mr. Morgan, and announced his intention.

JOE'S LUCK

"I don't think you will make money by your new plan, Joe," said Morgan.

"I don't expect to," said Joe, "but I want to see the mines. If I don't succeed I can come back to my business here."

"That is true. I should like very well to go, too."

"Why don't you, Mr. Morgan?"

"I cannot leave my business as readily as you can. Do you feel confidence in this man whom you are leaving in charge?"

"Yes, sir. He has been unlucky, but I am sure he is honest."

"He will have considerable money belonging to you by the time you return—that is, if you stay any length of time."

"I want to speak to you about that, Mr. Morgan. I have directed him to make a statement to you once a month, and put in your hands what money comes to me—if it won't trouble you too much."

"Not at all, Joe. I shall be glad to be of service to you."

"If you meet with any good investment for the money while I am away, I should like to have you act for me as you would for yourself."

"All right, Joe."

Joe learned from Watson that the latter had been mining on the Yuba River, not far from the town of Marysville. He decided to go there, although he might have found mines nearer the city. The next question was, how should he get there, and should he go alone?

About this time a long, lank Yankee walked into

the restaurant, one day, and seating himself at a table, began to inspect the bill of fare which Joe used to write up every morning. He looked disappointed.

"Don't you find what you want?" inquired Joe.

"No," said the visitor. "I say this is a queer country. I've been hankerin' arter a good dish of baked beans for a week, and ain't found any."

"We sometimes have them," said Joe. "Come here at one o'clock and you shall be accommodated."

"That's the talk," said he. "I'll come."

"Have you just come out here?" asked Joe, curiously.

"A week ago. I was raised in Pumpkin Hollow, State of Maine. I was twenty-one last first of April, but I ain't no April fool, I tell you. Dad and me carried on the farm till I began to hear tell of Californy. I'd got about three hundred dollars saved up, and I took it to come out here."

"I suppose you've come out to make your fortune?"

"Yes, sir-ee, that's just what I come for."

"How have you succeeded so far?"

"I've succeeded in spendin' all my money except fifty dollars. I say, it costs a sight to eat and drink out here. I can't afford to take but one meal a day, and then I eat like all possessed."

"I should think you would, Mr.——"

"Joshua Bickford—that's my name when I'm to hum."

"Well, Mr. Bickford, what are your plans?"

"I want to go out to the mines and dig gold. I guess I can dig as well as anybody. I've had experience in diggin' ever since I was ten year old."

"Not digging gold, I suppose?"

"Diggin' potatoes and sich."

"I'm going to the mines myself, Mr. Bickford. What do you say to going along with me?"

"I'm on hand. You know the way don't you?"

"We can find it, I have do doubt. I have never been there, but my friend, Mr. Watson, is an experienced miner."

"How much gold did you dig?" asked Joshua, bluntly.

"Two thousand dollars," answered Watson, not thinking it necessary to add that he had parted with the money since at the gaming-table.

"Two thousand dollars?" exclaimed Joshua, duly impressed. "That's a heap of money."

"Yes, it's a pretty good pile."

"I'd like to get that much. I know what I'd do."

"What would you do, Mr. Bickford?"

"I'd go home and marry Sukey Smith, by gosh."

"Then I hope you'll get the money for Miss Smith's sake."

"There's a feller hangin' round her," said Joshua, but if I come home with two thousand dollars, she'll have me, I guess. Why, with two thousand dollars I can buy the farm next to dad's, with a house with five rooms into it, and a good-sized barn. I guess Sukey wouldn't say no to me then, but would change her name to Bickford mighty sudden."

"I hope you will succeed in your plans, Mr. Bickford."

"Seems to me you're kinder young to be out here."

JOE'S LUCK

"Yes, I am not quite old enough to think of marrying."

"Have you got money enough to get out to the mines?"

"I think I can raise enough," said Joe, smiling.

"My young friend is the owner of this restaurant," said Watson.

"You don't say! I thought you hired him."

"No. On the contrary, I am in his employ. I have agreed to run the restaurant for him while he is at the mines."

"You don't say!" exclaimed Bickford, surveying our hero with curiosity. "Have you made much money in this eatin'-house?"

"I've done pretty well," said Joe, modestly. "I own the building and the two adjoining lots."

"Well, I guess Californy's the place to make money. I ain't made any yet, but I mean to. There wasn't no chance to get ahead in Pumpkin Hollow. I was workin' for eight dollars a month and board."

"It would be a great while before you could save up money to buy a farm out of that, Mr. Bickford."

By this time Mr. Bickford had completed his breakfast, and in an anxious tone he inquired:

"What's the damage?"

"Oh, I won't charge you anything, as you are going to be my traveling companion," said Joe.

"You're a gentleman, by gosh!"

"Come at one o'clock and you shall have some of your favorite beans and nothing to pay. Can you start for the mines to-morrow?"

"Yes—I've got nothin' to prepare."

JOE'S LUCK

"Take your meals here till we go."

"Well, I'm in luck," said Bickford. "Victuals cost awful out here, and I haven't had as much as I wanted to eat since I got here."

"Consider yourself my guest," said Joe, "and eat all you want to."

It may be remarked that Mr. Bickford availed himself of our young hero's invitation, and during the next twenty-four hours stowed away enough provisions to last an ordinary man for half a week.

Four days later Joe and his Yankee friend, mounted on mustangs, were riding through a canyon a hundred miles from San Francisco. It was late in the afternoon, and the tall trees shaded the path on which they were traveling. The air was unusually chilly, and after the heat of mid-day they felt it.

"I don't feel like campin' out to-night," said Bickford. "It's too cool."

"I don't think we shall find any hotels about here," said Joe.

"Don't look like it. I'd like to be back in Pumpkin Hollow just for to-night. How fur is it to the mines, do you calculate?"

"We are probably about half-way. We ought to reach the Yuba River inside of a week."

Here Mr. Bickford's mustang deliberately stopped and began to survey the scenery calmly.

"What do you mean, you pesky critter? G'lang!" said Joshua, and he brought down his whip on the flanks of the animal.

It is not in mustang nature to submit to such an outrage without expressing proper resentment. The animal threw up his hind legs, lowering his head at the same time, and Joshua Bickford, describing a sudden somersault, found himself sitting down on the ground a few feet in front of his horse, not seriously injured but considerably bewildered.

"Why didn't you tell me you were going to dismount, Mr. Bickford?" asked Joe, his eyes twinkling with merriment.

"Because I didn't know it myself," said Joshua, rising and rubbing his jarred frame.

The mustang did not offer to run away, but stood calmly surveying him as if it had had nothing to do with his rider's sudden dismounting.

"Darn the critter! He looks just as if nothing had happened," said Joshua. "He served me a mean trick."

"It was a gentle hint that he was tired," said Joe.

"Darn the beast! I don't like his hints."

He prepared to mount the animal, but the latter rose on his hind legs, and very clearly intimated that the proposal was not agreeable.

"What's got into the critter?" said Joshua.

"He wants to rest. Suppose we rest here for half an hour, while we loosen check-rein and let the horses graze."

"Just as you say."

Joshua's steed appeared pleased with the success of his little hint, and lost no time in availing himself of the freedom accorded him.

"I wish I was safe at the mines," said Joshua. "What would dad say if he knowed where I was, right out here in the wilderness? It looks as we might be the only human critters in the world. There ain't no house in sight, nor any signs of man's ever bein' here. There ain't no suspicious characters round, are there?" inquired Joshua, anxiously.

"We are liable to meet them—men who have been unsuccessful at the mines and who have become desperate in consequence, and others who came out here to prey upon others. That's what I hear."

"Do you think we shall meet any of the critters?" asked Joshua.

"I hope not. They wouldn't find it very profitable to attack us. We haven't much money."

"I haven't," said Joshua. "I couldn't have got to the mines if you hadn't lent me a few dollars."

"You have your animal. You can sell him for something."

"If he agrees to carry me so far," said Mr. Bickford, gazing doubtfully at the mustang, who was evidently enjoying his evening repast.

"Oh, a hearty meal will make him good-natured. That is the way it acts with boys and men, and animals are not so very different."

"I guess you're right," said Joshua. "When I wanted to get a favor out of dad, I always used to wait till the old man had got his belly full. That made him kinder good-natured."

"I see you understand human nature, Mr. Bickford," said Joe.

"We may as well be going," said Joe.

"Just as you say, Joe," said Joshua. "Here, you pesky critter, come and let me mount you."

The mustang realized Joe's prediction. After his

hearty supper he seemed to be quite tractable, and permitted Mr. Bickford to mount him without opposition.

Joe also mounted his horse.

CHAPTER XIII

ON THE YUBA RIVER

They rode on for about an hour and a half. Joshua's steed, placated by his good supper, behaved very well. Their ride was still through the canyon. Presently it became too dark for them to proceed.

"Ain't we gone about far enough for to-night?" asked Joshua.

"Perhaps we have," answered Joe.

"Here's a good place to camp."

"Very well; let us dismount," said Joe. "I think we can pass the night comfortably."

They dismounted and tied their beasts together under one of the trees. They then threw themselves down on a patch of greensward near by.

"I'm gettin' hungry," said Joshua. "Ain't you, Joe?"

"Yes, Mr. Bickford. We may as well take supper."

Mr. Bickford produced a supper of cold meat and bread, and placed it between Joe and himself.

"I wish we was to your restaurant, Joe," said Joshua. "I kinder hanker after some good baked beans. Baked beans and brown bread are scrumptious."

JOE'S LUCK

Supper was over and other subjects succeeded.
Conversation finally died away, and presently both were asleep.

On the following day Joe and his comrade fell in with a party of men who, like themselves, were on their way to the Yuba River. They were permitted to join them, and made an arrangement for a share of the provisions. This removed all anxiety and insured their reaching their destination without further adventure.

The banks of the Yuba presented a busy and picturesque appearance. On the banks was a line of men roughly clad, earnestly engaged in scooping out gravel and pouring it into a rough cradle, called a rocker. This was rocked from side to side until the particles of gold, if there were any, settled at the bottom and were picked out and gathered into bags. At present time there are improved methods of separating gold from the earth, but the rocker is still employed by Chinese miners.

In the background were tents and rude cabins, and there was the unfailing accessory of a large mining camp, the gambling tent, where the banker like a wily spider lay in wait to appropriate the hard-earned dust of the successful miner.

Joe and his friend took their station a few rods from the river and gazed at the scene before them.

"Well, Mr. Bickford," said Joe, "the time has come when we are to try our luck."

"Yes," said Joshua. "Looks curious, doesn't it? If I didn't know, I'd think them chaps fools, stoopin' over there and siftin' mud. It reminds me of when I was a boy and used to make dirt pies."

"Suppose we take a day and look round a little. Then we can find out how things are done and work to better advantage."

"Just as you say, Joe. I must go to work soon, for I hain't nary red."

Joe and his friend found the miners social and very ready to give them information.

"How much do I make a day?" said one in answer to a question from Joshua. "Well, it varies. Sometimes I make ten dollars, and from that all the way up to twenty-five. Once I found a piece worth fifty dollars. I was in luck then."

"I should say you were," said Mr. Bickford. "The idea of findin' fifty dollars in the river. It looks kind of strange, don't it, Joe?"

"Are any larger pieces ever found here?" asked Joe.

"Sometimes."

"I have seen large nuggets on exhibition in San Francisco worth several hundred dollars. Are any such to be found here?"

"Generally they come from the dry diggings. We don't often find such specimens in the river washings. But these are more reliable."

"Can a man save money here?"

"If he'll be careful of what he gets. But much of our dust goes there."

He pointed as he spoke to a small cabin, used as a store and gambling den at one and the same time. There in the evening the miners collected, and by

JOE'S LUCK

faro, poker or monte managed to lose all that they had washed out during the day.

"That's the curse of our mining settlement," said their informant. "But for the temptations which the gaming-house offers, many whom you see working here would now be on their way home with a comfortable provision for their families. I never go there but then I am in the minority."

"What did you used to do when you was to hum?" inquired Joshua, who was by nature curious and had no scruples about gratifying his curiosity.

"I used to keep school winters. In the spring and summer I assisted my father on his farm down in Maine."

"You don't say you're from Maine?" Why, I'm from Maine myself," remarked Joshua.

"Indeed! Whereabouts in Maine did you live?"

"Pumpkin Hollow."

"I kept school in Pumpkin Hollow one winter."

"You don't say so? What is your name?"

"John Kellogg."

"I thought so!" exclaimed Mr. Bickford, excited. "Why, I used to go to school to you, Mr. Kellogg."

"It is nine years ago, and you must have changed so much that I cannot call you to mind."

"Don't you remember a tall, slab-sided youngster of thirteen, that used to stick pins into your chair for you to set on?"

Kellogg smiled.

"Surely you are not Joshua Bickford?" he said.

"Yes, I am. I am that same identical chap."

"I am glad to see you, Mr. Bickford," said his old

school-teacher, grasping Joshua's hand cordially.

"It seems kinder queer for you to call me Mr. Bickford."

"I wasn't so ceremonious in the old times."

"No, I guess not. You'd say, 'Come here, Joshua,' and you'd jerk me out of my seat by the collar. 'Did you stick that pin in my chair?' That's the way you used to talk. And then you'd give me an all-fired lickin'."

Overcome by the mirthful recollections, Joshua burst into an explosive fit of laughter in which presently he was joined by Joe and his old teacher.

"I hope you've forgiven me for those whippings."

"They were jest what I needed, Mr. Kellogg. I was a lazy young rascal, as full of mischief as a nut is of meat. You tanned my hide well."

"You don't seem to be any the worse for it now."

"I guess not. I'm pretty tough. I say, Mr. Kellogg," continued Joshua, with a grin, "you'd find it a harder job to give me a lickin' now than you did then."

"I wouldn't undertake it now. I am afraid you could handle me."

"It seems cur'us, don't it, Joe?" said Joshua. "When Mr. Kellogg used to haul me round the schoolroom, it didn't seem as if I could ever be a match for him."

"We change with the passing of years," said Kellogg, in a moralizing tone, which recalled his former vocation. "Now you are a man, and we meet here on the other side of the continent on the banks of the Yuba River. I hope we are destined to be successful."

JOE'S LUCK

"I hope so, too," said Joshua, "for I'm reg'larly cleaned out."

"If I can help you any in the way of information I shall be glad to do so."

Joe and Bickford took him at his word and made many inquiries, eliciting important information.

The next day they took their places further down the river and commenced work.

Their inexperience at first put them at a disadvantage. They were awkward and unskillful, as might have been expected. Still, at the end of the first day each had made about five dollars.

"That's something," said Joe.

"If I could have made five dollars in one day in Pumpkin Hollow," said Mr. Bickford, "I would have felt like a rich man. Here it costs a feller so much to live that he don't think much of it."

"We shall improve as we go along. Wait till tomorrow night."

The second day brought each about twelve dollars, and Joshua felt elated.

"I'm gettin' the hand of it," said he. "As soon as I've paid up what I owe you, I'll begin to lay by something."

"I don't want you to pay me till you are worth five hundred dollars, Mr. Bickford. The sum is small, and I don't need it."

"Thank you, Joe. You're a good friend. I'll stick by you if you ever want help."

In the evening the camp presented a lively appearance.

When it was chilly, logs would be brought from

the woods, and a bright fire would be lighted, around which the miners would sit and talk of home and their personal adventures and experiences.

CHAPTER XIV

A GRIZZLY ON THE WARPATH

Three months passed. They were not eventful. The days were spent in steady and monotonous work; the nights were passed around the camp-fire, telling and hearing stories and talking of home. Most of their companions gambled and drank, but Mr. Bickford and Joe kept clear of these pitfalls.

"Come, man, drink with me," more than once one of his comrades said to Joshua.

"No thank you," said Joshua.

Joe was equally positive in declining to drink, but it was easier for him to escape. Even the most confirmed drinkers felt it to be wrong to coax a boy to drink against his will.

"Joshua," said Joe, some three months after their arrival, "have you taken account of stock lately?"

"No," said Joshua, "but I'll do it now."

After a brief time he announced the result.

"I've got about five hundred dollars, or thereabouts."

"You have done a little better than I have."

"How much have you?"

"About four hundred and fifty."

JOE'S LUCK

"I am getting rather tired of this place, Mr. Bickford."

"You don't think of going back to the city?"

"Not directly, but I think I should like to see a little more of California. These are not the only diggings."

"Where do you want to go?"

"I haven't considered yet. The main thing is will you go with me?"

"We won't part company, Joe."

"Good! Then I'll inquire and see what I can find out about other places. This pays fairly, but there is little chance of getting nuggets of any size hereabouts."

"I'd just like to find one worth two thousand dollars. I'd start for home mighty quick, and give Sukey Smith a chance to become Mrs. Bickford."

"Success to you!" said Joe, laughing.

Joe finally decided on some mines a hundred miles distant in a southwesterly direction. They were reported to be rich and promising.

"At any rate," said he, "even if they are no better than here, we shall get a little variety and change of scene."

"That'll be good for our appetite."

"I don't think, Mr. Bickford, that either of us need be concerned about his appetite. Mine is remarkably healthy."

"Nothing was ever the matter with mine," said Joshua, "as long as the provisions held out."

They made some few preparations of a neccessary character. Their clothing was in rags, and they got a new outfit at the mining-store. Each also provided himself with a rifle. The expense of these made some inroads upon their stock of money, but by the time they were ready to start they had eight hundred dollars between them, besides their outfit, and this they considered satisfactory.

Mr. Bickford and Joe had not disposed of their horses. They had suffered them to forage in the neighborhood of the river, thinking it possible that the time would come when they would require them.

One fine morning they set out from the camp near the banks of the Yuba and set their faces in a southwesterly direction. They had made themselves popular among their comrades, and the miners gave them a hearty cheer as they started.

"Good luck, Joe! Good luck, old man!" they exclaimed.

"The same to you, boys!"

So with mutual good feeling they parted company.

On the fourth day Joe suddenly exclaimed in excitement:

"Look, Joshua!"

"By gosh!"

The exclamation was a natural one. At a distance of forty rods a man was visible, his hat off, his face wild with fear, and in dangerous proximity a grizzly bear of the largest size doggedly pursuing him.

"It's Hogan!" exclaimed Joe, in surprise. "We must save him."

When Hogan first saw the grizzly there was a considerable space between them. If he had concealed himself he might have escaped the notice of the beast, but when he commenced running the grizzly became aware of his presence and started in pursuit.

Hogan was rather dilapidated in appearance. Trusting to luck instead of labor, he had had a hard time, as he might have expected. He was running rapidly, but was already showing signs of exhaustion. The bear was getting over the ground with clumsy speed, appearing to take it easily, but overhauling his intended victim slowly but surely.

Joe and Bickford were standing on one side, and had not yet attracted the attention of either party in this unequal race.

"Poor chap!" said Joshua. "He looks 'most tuckered out. Shall I shoot?"

"Wait till the bear gets a little nearer. We can't afford to miss. He will turn on us."

"I'm in a hurry to roll the beast over," said Joshua. "It's a cruel sight to see a grizzly hunting a man.

At this moment Hogan turned his head with the terror-stricken look of a man who felt that he was lost.

The bear was little more than a hundred feet behind him and was gaining steadily. He was already terribly fatigued—his breathing was reduced to a hoarse pant. He was overcome by the terror of the situation and his remaining strength gave way. With a shrill cry he sunk down upon the ground, and shutting his eyes awaited the attack.

The bear increased his speed.

"Now let him have it!" said Joe.

Mr. Bickford fired, striking the grizzly in the face.

JOE'S LUCK

Bruin stood still and roared angrily. He wagged his large head from one side to the other, seeking by whom this attack was made.

He espied the two friends, and abandoning his pursuit of Hogan, rolled angrily toward them.

"Give it to him quick, Joe!" exclaimed Bickford. "He's making for us."

Joe held his rifle with steady hand and took deliberate aim. It was well he did, for had he failed both he and Bickford would have been in great peril.

His faithful rifle did good service.

The bear tumbled to the earth with sudden awkwardness. The bullet had reached a vital part and the grizzly was destined to do no more mischief.

"Is he dead, or only feigning?" asked Joe, prudently.

"He's a gone 'coon," said Joshua. "Let us go up and look at him."

They went up and stood over the huge beast. He was not quite dead. He opened his glazing eyes, made a convulsive movement with his paws as if he would like to attack his foes, and then his head fell back and he moved no more.

"He's gone, sure enough," said Bickford. "Goodby, old grizzly. You meant well, but circumstances interfered with your good intentions."

"Now let's look up Hogan," said Joe.

The man had sunk to the ground utterly exhausted and in his weakness and terror had fainted.

Joe got some water and threw it in his face.

He opened his eyes and drew a deep breath. A

sudden recollection blanched his face anew, and he cried:

"Don't let him get at me!"

"You're safe, Mr. Hogan," said Joe. "The bear is dead."

"Dead! Is he really dead?"

"If you don't believe it get up and look at him," said Bickford.

Hogan shuddered as he caught sight of the huge beast only twenty-five feet distant from him.

"Was he as near as that?" he gasped.

"He almost had you," said Bickford. "If it hadn't been for Joe and me he'd have been munchin' you at this identical minute. Things have changed a little, and in place of the bear eatin' you, you shall help eat the bear."

By this time Hogan, realizing that he was safe, began to recover his strength. As he did so he became angry with the beast that had given him such a hard race for life. He ran up to the grizzly and kicked him.

"Take that!" he exclaimed with an oath. "I wish you wasn't dead so that I could stick my knife into you."

"If he wasn't dead you'd keep your distance," said Joshua, dryly. "It don't require much courage to tackle him now."

Hogan felt this to be a reflection upon his courage.

"I guess you'd have run, too, if he'd been after you."

"I guess I should. Bears are all very well in their

place, but I'd rather not mingle with 'em socially. They're very affectionate and fond of hugging, but if I'm going to be hugged I wouldn't choose a bear."

"You seem to think I was a coward for runnin' from the bear."

"No, I don't. How do I know you was runnin' from the bear? Maybe you was only takin' a little exercise to get up an appetite for dinner."

"I am faint and weak," said Hogan. "I haven't had anything to eat for twelve hours."

"You shall have some food," said Joe. "Joshua, where are the provisions? We may as well sit down and lunch."

"Jest as you say, Joe. I most generally have an appetite."

There was a mountain spring within a stone's-throw. Joshua took a tin pail and brought some of the sparkling beverage, which he offered first to Hogan.

Hogan drank greedily. His throat was parched and dry, and he needed it.

He drew a deep breath of relief.

"I feel better," said he. "I was in search of a spring when that cursed beast spied me and gave me chase."

They sat down under the shade of a large tree and lunched.

"What sort of luck have you had since you tried to break into my restaurant, Mr. Hogan?" asked Joe.

"Who told you I tried to enter your restaurant?"

"The man you brought there."

JOE'S LUCK

"That wasn't creditable of you, Hogan," said Joshua, with his mouth full. "After my friend Joe had given you a supper and promised you breakfast, it was unkind to try to rob him. Don't you think so yourself?"

"I couldn't help it," said Hogan.

"Couldn't help it?" said Joe, in a tone of inquiry. "That's rather a strange statement."

"It's true," said Hogan. "The man forced me to do it."

"How was that?"

"He saw me comin' out of the restaurant a little while before, and when he met me after trying to rob me and finding that it didn't pay, he asked me if I was a friend of yours. I told him I was. Then he began to ask if you slept there at night and if anybody was with you. I didn't want to answer, but he held a pistol at my head and forced me to. Then he made me go with him. I offered to get in, thinking I could whisper in your ear and warn you, but he wouldn't let me. He stationed me at the window and got in himself. You know what followed. As soon as I saw you were too strong for him I ran away, fearing that he might try to implicate me in the attempt at robbery."

Hogan recited this story very glibly and in a very plausible manner.

"Mr. Hogan," said Joe, "if I didn't know you so thoroughly I might be disposed to put confidence in your statements. As it is, I regret to say I don't believe you."

CHAPTER XV

THE NEW DIGGINGS

When lunch was over, Joe said:

"Good-day, Mr. Hogan. Look out for the grizzlies, and may you have better luck in the future."

"Yes, Hogan, good-by," said Joshua. "We make over to you our interest in the bear. He meant to eat you. You can revenge yourself by eatin' him."

"Are you going to leave me, gentlemen?" asked Hogan.

"You don't expect us to stay and take care of you, do you?"

"Let me go with you," pleaded Hogan. "I am afraid to be left alone in this country. I may meet another grizzly and lose my life."

"That would be a great loss to the world."

"Mr. Hogan," said Joe, "you know very well why your company is not acceptable to us."

"You shall have no occasion to complain," said Hogan.

Joe turned to Bickford.

"If you don't object," he said, "I think I'll let him come."

"Let the critter come," said Bickford.

As they advanced the country became rougher and more hilly. Here and there they saw evidences of "prospecting" by former visitors. They came upon deserted claims and the sites of former camps. But

JOE'S LUCK

in these places the indications of gold had not been sufficiently favorable to warrant continued work, and the miners had gone elsewhere.

At last, however, they came to a dozen men who were busily at work in a gulch. Two rude huts near by evidently served as their temporary homes.

"Well, boys, how do you find it?" inquired Bickford.

"Pretty fair," said one of the party.

"Have you got room for three more?"

"Yes—come along. You can select claims alongside and go to work if you want to."

"What do you say, Joe?"

"I am in favor of it."

"We are going to put up here, Hogan," said Mr. Bickford. "You can do as you've a mind to. Much as we value your interestin' society, we hope you won't put yourself out to stay on our account."

"I'll stay," said Hogan.

Joe and Joshua surveyed the ground and staked out their claims, writing out the usual notice and posting it on a neighboring tree. They had not all the requisite tools, but these they were able to purchase at one of the cabins.

"What shall I do?" asked Hogan. "I'm dead-broke. I can't work without tools, and I can't buy any."

"Do you want to work for me?" asked Joshua.

"What'll you give?"

"That'll depend on how you work. If you work stiddy, I'll give you a quarter of what we both make. I'll supply you with tools, but they'll belong to me."

JOE'S LUCK

"Suppose we don't make anything?" asked Hogan.

"You shall have a quarter of that. You see, I want to make it for your interest to succeed."

"Then I shall starve."

The bargain was modified so that Hogan was assured of enough to eat, and was promised besides, a small sum of money daily, but was not to participate in the gains.

"If we find a nugget it won't do you any good. Do you understand, Hogan?"

"Yes, I understand."

On the second day Joe and Mr. Bickford consolidated their claims and became partners, agreeing to divide whatever they found. Hogan was to work for them jointly.

They did not find their hired man altogether satisfactory. He was lazy and shiftless by nature, and work was irksome to him.

"If you don't work stiddy, Hogan," said Joshua "you can't expect to eat stiddy, and your appetite is pretty reg'lar, I notice."

Under this stimulus Hogan managed to work better than he had done since he came to California, or indeed for years preceding his departure. Bickford and Joe had both been accustomed to farm work and easily lapsed into their old habits.

They found they had made a change for the better in leaving the banks of the Yuba. The claims they were now working paid them better.

"Twenty-five dollars to-day," said Joshua, a week after their arrival. "That pays better than hoeing pertaters."

JOE'S LUCK

"You are right, Mr. Bickford. You are ten dollars ahead of me. I am afraid you will lose on our partnership."

"I'll risk it, Joe."

Hogan was the only member of the party who was not satisfied.

"Can't you take me into partnership?" he asked.

"We can, but I don't think we will Hogan."

"Mr. Hogan, if you want to start a claim of your own I'll give you what tools you need," said Joe.

Upon reflection Hogan decided to accept this offer.

"But of course you will have to find your own vittles now," said Joshua.

"I'll do it," said Hogan.

The same day he ceased to work for the firm of Bickford & Mason, for Joe insisted on giving Mr. Bickford the precedence as the senior party, and started on his own account.

The result was that he worked considerably less than before. Being his own master he decided not to overwork himself, and in fact worked only enough to make his board. He was continually grumbling over his bad luck, although Joshua told him plainly that it wasn't luck but industry he lacked.

"If you'd work like we do," said Bickford, "you wouldn't need to complain. Your claim is just as good as ours as far as we can tell."

About this time a stroke of good luck fell to Joe. About three o'clock one afternoon he unearthed a nugget which at a rough estimate might be worth five hundred dollars.

Instantly all was excitement in the mining camp,

JOE'S LUCK

not alone for what he had obtained, but for the promise of richer deposits. Experienced miners decided that he had struck upon what is popularly called a "pocket," and some of these are immensely remunerative.

"Shake hands, Joe," said Bickford. "You're in luck."

"So are you, Mr. Bickford. We are partners, you know."

In less than an hour the two partners received an offer of eight thousand dollars for their united claim, and the offer was accepted.

Joe was the hero of the camp. All were rejoiced at his good fortune except one. That one was Hogan, who from a distance, jealous and gloomy, surveyed the excited crowd.

The parties to whom Joe and his partner sold their claim were responsible men who had been fortunate in mining and had a bank account in San Francisco.

"We'll give you an order on our banker," they proposed.

"That will suit me better than money down," said Joe. "I shall start for San Francisco to-morrow, having other business there that I need to look after."

"I'll go too, Joe," said Joshua. "With my share of the purchase money and the nugget, I'm worth nigh on to five thousand dollars. What will dad say?"

"And what will Susan Smith say?" queried Joe.

"I guess she'll say she's ready to change her name to Bickford," said he.

Joe observed with some surprise that Hogan did not come near them. The rest without exception had

JOE'S LUCK

congratulated them on their extraordinary good luck.

"Seems to me Hogan looks rather down in the mouth," said Joe to Bickford.

"He's mad 'cause he didn't find the nugget. That's what's the matter with him. I say, Hogan, you look as if your dinner didn't agree with you."

"My luck don't agree with me. I'd give something for that boy's luck."

"Joe's luck? Well, things have gone pretty well with him; but that don't explain all his success—he's willin' to work."

"So am I."

"Then go to work on your claim. There's no knowin' but there's a bigger nugget inside of it. If you stand round with your hands in your pockets you'll never find it."

"It's the poorest claim in the gulch," said Hogan.

"It pays the poorest because you don't work half the time."

Hogan apparently didn't like Mr. Bickford's plainness of speech. He walked away moodily, with his hands in his pockets. He could not help contrasting his penniless position with the enviable position of the two friends, and the devil who is always in wait for such moments, thrust an evil suggestion into his mind.

He asked himself why could he not steal the nugget which Joe had found?

"I'll try for it," Hogan decided, "this very night."

CHAPTER XVI

THE NUGGET IS STOLEN

They retired in good season, for they wished to start early on their journey on the following morning.

"I don't know as I can go to sleep," said Joshua. "I can't help thinkin' of how rich I am, and what dad and all the folks will say."

"Do you mean to go home at once, Mr. Bickford?"

"Jest as soon as I can get ready. I'll tell you what I am goin' to do, Joe. I'm goin' to buy a tip-top suit when I get to Boston, and a gold watch and chain, and a breastpin about as big as a saucer. When I sail into Pumpkin Holler in that rig folks'll look at me, you bet. There's old Squire Pennyroyal, he'll be disapp'inted for one?"

"Why will he be disappointed?"

"Because he told dad I was a fool to come out here. He said I'd be back in rags before a year was out. Now, the old man thinks a good deal of his opinion, and he won't like it to find how badly he's mistaken."

"How about Susan? Ain't you afraid she has married the store clerk?"

"I won't say but she has," said he; "but if she has gone and forgotten about me because my back is turned, she ain't the gal I take her for, and I won't fret my gizzard about her."

"What are your plans, Joe? Shall you remain in San Francisco?"

JOE'S LUCK

"I've been thinking, Mr. Bickford, that I would like to go home on a visit. If I find I have left my business in good hands in the city, I shall feel strongly tempted to go home on the same steamer with you."

"That would be hunky," said Bickford, really delighted. "We'd have a jolly time."

While this conversation was going on the dark figure of a man was prowling near the tent.

The two friends ceased talking and lay quite still. Soon Joe's deep, regular breathing and Bickford's snoring convinced the listener that the time had come to carry out his plans.

With stealthy step he approached the tent, and stooping over gently removed the nugget from under Joshua's head. There was a bag of gold-dust which escaped his notice. The nugget was all he thought of.

With beating heart and hasty step the thief melted into the darkness, and the two friends slept on unconscious of their loss.

The sun was up an hour before Joe and Bickford awoke. When Joe opened his eyes he saw that it was later than the hour he intended to rise. He shook his companion.

"Is it mornin'?" asked Bickford, drowsily.

"I should say it was. Everybody is up and eating breakfast. We must prepare to set out on our journey."

"Then it is time—we are rich," said Joshua, with sudden remembrance. "Do you know, Joe, I hain't got used to the idea yet. I had actually forgotten it."

JOE'S LUCK

"The sight of the nugget will bring it to mind."

"That's so."

Bickford felt for the nugget, without suspicion that the search would be vain.

Of course he did not find it.

"Joe you are trying to play a trick on me," he said. "You've taken the nugget."

"What!" exclaimed Joe, starting. "Is it really missing?"

"Yes, and you know all about it."

"On my honor, Joshua, I haven't touched it," said Joe, seriously. "Where did you place it?"

"Under my head—the last thing before I lay down."

"Then," said Joe, a little pale, "it must have been taken during the night."

"Who would take it?"

"Let us find Hogan," said Joe, with instinctive suspicion. "Who has seen Hogan?"

Hogan's claim was in sight, but he was not at work. Neither was he taking breakfast.

"I'll bet the skunk has grabbed the nugget and cleared out," exclaimed Bickford, in a tone of conviction.

"Did you hear or see anything of him during the night?"

"No—I slept too sound."

"Is anything else taken?" asked Joe. "The bag of dust—"

"Is safe. It's only the nugget that's gone."

The loss was quickly noised about the camp. Such an incident was of common interest. Miners lived so much in common—their property was necessarily left so unguarded—that theft was something more than misdemeanor or light offense. Stern was the justice which overtook the thief in those days. It was necessary perhaps, for it was a primitive state of society, and the code which in established communities was a safeguard did not extend its protection here.

Suspicion fell upon Hogan at once. No one of the miners remembered to have seen him since rising.

"Did anyone see him last night?" asked Joe.

"I saw him near your tent," said one. "I did not think anything of it. Perhaps if I had been less sleepy I should have been more likely to suspect that his design was not a good one."

"About what hour was this?"

"It must have been between ten and eleven o'clock."

"We did not go to sleep at once. Mr. Bickford and I were talking over our plans."

"I wish I'd been awake when the skunk come round," said Bickford. "I'd have grabbed him so he'd thought an old grizzly'd got hold of him."

"Did you notice anything in his manner that led you to think he intended robbery?"

"He was complainin' of his luck. He thought Joe and I got more than our share, and I'm willin' to allow we have; but if we'd been as lazy and shif'less as Hogan we wouldn't have got down to the nugget at all."

An informal council was held, and it was decided to pursue Hogan. As it was uncertain in which direction he had fled, it was resolved to send out four parties of two men each to hunt him. Joe and one miner went together, Joshua and another miner departed in a different direction, and two other pairs started out.

"I guess we'll fix him," said Mr. Bickford. "If he can dodge us all he's smarter than I think he is."

Meanwhile Hogan, with the precious nugget in his possession, hurried forward with feverish haste. The night was dark and the country was broken. From time to time he stumbled over some obstacle, the root of a tree or something similar, and this made his journey more arduous.

He stumbled on, occasionally forced by his fatigue to sit down and rest.

He had been traveling with occasional rests for four hours when fatigue overcame him. He lay down to take a slight nap, but when he awoke the sun was up.

"They have just discovered their loss," thought Hogan. "Will they follow me, I wonder. I must be a good twelve miles away, and this is a fair start. They will turn back before they have come as far as this. Besides, they won't know in what direction I have come."

About eleven o'clock Hogan sat down to rest. He reclined on the greensward near the edge of a precipitous descent. He did not dream that danger was so close till he heard his name called and two men came running toward him. Hogan, starting to his feet in dismay, recognized Crane and Peabody, two of his late comrades.

JOE'S LUCK

"What do you want?" he faltered.

"The nugget," said Crane, sternly.

Hogan would have denied its possession if he could, but there it was at his side.

"There it is," he said.

"What induced you to steal it?" demanded Crane.

"I was dead-broke. Luck was against me. I couldn't help it."

"It was a bad day's work for you," said Peabody. "Didn't you know the penalty attached to theft in the mining camps?"

"No," faltered Hogan, alarmed at the stern looks of his captors. "What is it?"

"Death by hanging," was the terrible reply.

Hogan's face blanched, and he sunk on his knees before them.

"Don't let me be hung!" he entreated. "You've got the nugget back. I've done no harm. No one has lost anything by me."

"Eight of us have lost our time in pursuing you. You gave up the nugget because you were forced to. You intended to carry it away."

"Mercy! mercy! I'm a very unlucky man. I'll go away and never trouble you again."

"We don't mean that you shall," said Crane, sternly. "Peabody, tie his hands; we must take him back with us."

"I won't go," said Hogan, lying down. "I'm not going back to be hung."

"We must hang you on the spot then," said Crane, producing a cord. "Say your prayers; your fate is sealed."

JOE'S LUCK

He advanced toward Hogan, who now felt the full horrors of his situation. He sprung to his feet, rushed in frantic fear to the edge of the precipice, threw up his ams, and plunged headlong. It was done so quickly that neither of his captors was able to prevent him.

They hurried to the precipice and looked over. A hundred feet below, on a rough rock, they saw a shapeless and motionless figure, crushed out of human semblance.

"Perhaps it is as well," said Crane, gravely. "He has saved us an unwelcome task."

The nugget was restored to its owners, to whom Hogan's tragical fate was told.

CHAPTER XVII

HOW JOE'S BUSINESS PROSPERED

Joe and his friend Bickford arrived in San Francisco eight days later without having met with any other misadventure or drawback. He had been absent less than three months, yet he found changes. A considerable number of buildings had gone up in different parts of the town during his absence.

"It is a wonderful place," said Joe to his companion. "It is going to be a great city some day."

Of course Joe's first visit was to his old place of business. He received a hearty greeting from Watson.

JOE'S LUCK

"I am glad to see you, Joe," said he, grasping our hero's hand cordially. "When did you arrive?"

"Ten minutes ago. I have made you the first call."

"Perhaps you thought I might have 'vamoosed the ranch,'" said Watson, smiling, "and left you and the business in the lurch."

"I had no fears on that score," said Joe. "Has business been good?"

"Excellent. I have paid weekly your share of the profits to Mr. Morgan."

"Am I a millonaire yet?" asked Joe.

"Not quite. I have paid Mr. Morgan on your account (here Watson consulted a small account-book) nine hundred and twenty-five dollars."

"Is it possible?" said Joe, gratified. "That is splendid."

"I am glad of it. I have made the same for myself, and so have nearly half made up the sum which I so foolishly squandered at the gaming-table."

"I am glad for you, Mr. Watson."

"How have you prospered at the mines?"

"I have had excellent luck."

"I don't believe you bring home as much money as I have made for you here."

"Don't bet on that, Mr. Watson, for you would lose."

"You don't mean to say that you have made a thousand dollars?" exclaimed Watson, surprised.

"I have made five thousand dollars within a hundred or two."

"Is it possible!" ejaculated Watson. "You beat everything for luck, Joe."

JOE'S LUCK

"So he does," said Bickford, who felt that it was time for him to speak. "It's lucky for me that I fell in with him. It brought me luck, too, for we went into partnership together."

"Have you brought home five thousand dollars, too?"

"I've got about the same as Joe, and now I'm going home to marry Susan Smith if she'll have me."

"She'll marry a rich miner, Mr. Bickford. You needn't be concerned about that."

Watson turned to Joe.

"I suppose you will now take charge of your own business?" said he. "I am ready to hand over my trust at any minute."

"Would you object to retaining charge for—say for four months to come?" asked Joe.

"Object? I should be delighted to do it. I couldn't expect to make as much money any other way."

"You see, Mr. Watson, I am thinking of going home myself on a visit. I feel that I can afford it, and I should like to see my old friends and acquaintances under my new and improved circumstances."

"You may depend upon it that your interests are safe in my hands," said he. "I will carry on the business as if it were my own. Indeed, it will be for my interest to do so."

"I don't doubt it, Mr. Watson. I have perfect confidence in your management."

Joe's next call was on his friend Morgan, by whom also he was cordially welcomed.

"Have you called on Watson?' he asked.

"Yes."

JOE'S LUCK

"Then he has probably given you an idea of how your business has gone on during your absence. He is a thoroughly reliable man in my opinion. You were fortunate to secure his services."

"So I think."

"Have you done well at the mines?" asked Mr. Morgan, doubtfully.

"You hope so, but you don't feel confident?" said Joe, smiling.

"You can read my thoughts exactly. I don't consider mining as reliable as a regular business."

"Nor I, in general, but there is one thing you don't take into account."

"What is that?"

Mr. Bickford answered the question.

"Joe's luck."

"Then you have been lucky?"

"How much do you think I have brought home?"

"A thousand dollars?"

"Five times that sum."

"Are you in earnest?" asked Mr. Morgan, incredulous.

"Wholly so."

"Then let me congratulate you—on that and something else."

"What is that?"

"The lots you purchased, including the one on which your restaurant is situated, have more than doubled in value."

"Bully for you, Joe!" exclaimed Mr. Bickford.

"It never rains but it pours," said Joe, quoting

an old proverb. "I begin to think I shall be rich some time, Mr. Morgan."

Comparatively wealthy as Joe was, it would not have been such reckless extravagance for both him and Joshua to board at one of the best hotels during the time they were forced to remain in San Francisco waiting for a steamer, but neither cared to indulge in so much luxury.

"We've kinder got broke in to roughin' it, an' it won't hurt us to work the same vein a while longer," Mr. Bickford replied, when Joe broached the subject.

"That is my opinion. There's plenty of room for us to sleep at the restaurant, and we may as well save our money."

"You're right, Joe."

Watson, now he was assured he could hold the business four months longer, felt highly delighted at entertaining the two visitors, and promised Joshua that he should have pork and beans as many times as there were days in the week.

"I'll keep a pot in the oven all the time," he said.

The first stroll in the city after his return from the mine, caused Joe no slight amount of pleasure, for it enabled him to pay a debt which had been troubling him not a little.

As he and Joshua were walking past the Leidesdorff House, eyeing curiously a party of would-be miners who had just arrived from the East, a young gentleman emerged from the hotel, and came to a full stop on seeing Joe.

"It strikes me you were my room-mate on the steamer Columbus."

JOE'S LUCK

"Indeed I was, sir, thanks to the generosity of yourself and Mr. Scudder."

"Where have you been all this time? Judging from appearances, which is by no means safe out here, you haven't made a fortune yet."

"I have got a good start toward it, at all events," Joe replied, with a laugh. "Will you allow me to introduce a friend of mine, Mr. Joshua Bickford?"

"I am glad to meet you, sir," Folsom said as he took the outstretched hand and submitted to a pressure which made the very bones crack. "Are you from the East?"

"Come from way down in Maine, where they shove the sun up with a crow-bar. Pumpkin Holler. I'll be spreadin' myself over the town before long."

"Made your pile, eh?"

"Wa'al Joe an' me have brought back nigh on to ten thousand dollars."

"Is this true, Joe?" Folsom asked in surprise.

"Yes," was the modest reply, "I have been very fortunate, and I owe it all to you and Mr. Scudder."

"I knew you would come out a winner, my boy."

"Thank you, sir, and now I want to pay the hundred dollars I owe to Mr. Scudder."

"It is no more than right to do so, although it would not have worried him very much if he had never received it. Come in here, and we can soon straighten matters."

Entering the hotel, Folsom procured paper, ink and pen, with which he made out a receipt for the hundred dollars paid him for Richard Scudder, and Joe was finally free from debt.

JOE'S LUCK

"Now, Mr. Folsom," the latter said, hesitatingly, when the money had been paid, "will you do me one more favor?"

"Certainly. What is it?"

"I want to give you something which you can show as coming from a grateful boy to whom you stood a good friend when he was in trouble. I'm not thinkof the value; but only that I dug it myself, and shall be very happy if you'll accept it."

"As he spoke Joe took from his pouch a nugget weighing about two ounces, and in form not unlike a rose half blown.

"Why, it is beautiful, Joe!" Folsom cried, delighted, "and I am more than pleased at receiving it. I shall prize the nugget very highly, and when my friends ask its history, I will say it was given me by an honest boy, who deserved all the good fortune which has come to him."

"Come down to my restaurant before we sail.'

"I shall most certainly accept your invitation," Folsom replied, and after a hearty hand-shake he walked away, leaving the partners to continue their interrupted stroll.

Sight-seeing is oftentimes as fatiguing as actual work, however, and when night came both were more than glad to return to the restaurant where, true to his promise, Watson had already a pot of steaming beans, and a huge pile of fish-cakes for Joshua's especial benefit.

The restaurant was yet well filled with customers when the two retired to the pantry, as it was called, although it served as general store-room and woodshed, and here Joshua stretched himself out on a thin bed to take, as he expressed it, "solid comfort."

CHAPTER XVIII

HOMEWARD BOUND

Joe had fancied that six days would be none too long in which to "see the sights" of the city; but when two had passed he was impatient to be on his way home. It is not to be wondered at that he was eager to show himself in Oakville as a person of considerable wealth, considering the circumstances under which he left, and now that all his business had been transacted, every day spent in San Francisco seemed like just so much time wasted.

Finally the longed-for day arrived, as all days will, whether they bring joy or sorrow, and the two successful miners went on board the steamer, occupying one of the best state-rooms.

On the steamer's deck was a motley crowd of gold-seekers returning home, and it was easy to say which were the successful members of the party.

Nearly all wore the garb of the mining camp; but here and there was one, who, having suddenly come into possession of great wealth, advertised the fact by arraying himself in "store clothes," purchased at an enormous price, and affording a marked contrast to the bronzed face and toil-hardened hands.

The good-fellowship of the mines prevented anything like restraint among the passengers No one

JOE'S LUCK

appeared to think it rude when another asked if he had "struck it rich," and without hesitation told exactly the size of the "pile" he was carrying home. Thus Joe learned that the man who occupied the next room to his had found a nugget valued at twenty thousand dollars in a claim which had been abandoned, and worked by him because he did not have the capital with which to buy the one he wanted. Another told, and the story was vouched for by several on board, of taking out twelve thousand dollars' worth of small nuggets from one hole in two days, while a third boasted of having dug thirty pounds of coarse gold in a week.

There were very many who had gotten comparatively small amounts, as in the cases of Joe and Mr. Bickford, and quite as many more who were obliged to send home for funds with which to pay their passage money.

"We're a good deal better off than many of this crowd," Joshua whispered to Joe, while the miners were telling their stories; "but how Susan's eyes would a' stuck out if I'd got that twenty thousand dollar nugget."

"That is true; but you should feel rich when you think of those aboard who got nothing for their hard work, and, in addition, lost all they brought out here."

This last idea caused Mr. Bickford to look at the matter in a very different light, and from that moment no one ever heard him express any dissatisfaction, or desire to return to the diggings.

With both the travelers in whom we are interested,

in such a happy frame of mind, it is not to be wondered at that the time passed rapidly, and Joe could hardly realize he had been so long on shipboard when it was announced that they would land at the Isthmus the following day.

To Joe the short journey across the Isthmus was very interesting. The railroad which had cost so many lives during construction, seemed to have a dreadful fascination for him, and he looked intently from the car window the entire time, regardless of Joshua's innocent chatter about Susan.

The quarters assigned them for the trip up the coast were even more comfortable than those just left, and Joe said, with a sigh of relief, after making sure all their baggage was on board:

"When we step off this steamer I shall be very near Oakville, and it will be as if the journey to California was nothing more than a dream."

"I'd like to have a lot of sich dreams, if they'd bring in five thousand dollars," Joshua replied with a chuckle of satisfaction. "There's nothin' like the ring of hard cash to tell a feller that he's been awake an' workin'."

With the exception of what the captain called "half a gale of wind," no heavy weather was encountered, and the dreaded passage around Hatteras was such a very tame affair that but few really knew when it had been accomplished.

Then came the night when men said to each other, "To-morrow we shall be in New York," and the saloon-lamps were left burning until a late hour as

JOE'S LUCK

the passengers celebrated, with more liquor than wit, the happy ending of the voyage.

Big bowls of punch were brewed, and a general invitation was extended by the more fortunate miners to all hands, in order, as one said:

"To wind up in ship-shape fashion the race for gold."

Neither Joe nor Mr. Bickford participated in the festivities. They belonged to the "Cold Water Brigade," and were perfectly willing to "wind" the race up by going to bed.

On arriving in New York both Joe and Mr. Bickford bought new suits of clothes.

It is not my purpose to describe Mr. Bickford's arrival in Pumpkin Hollow, resplendent in his new suit. Joshua wouldn't have exchanged places with the President of the United States on that day. His old friends gathered about him, and listened open-mouthed to his stories of mining life in California and his own wonderful exploits, which lost nothing in the telling. He found his faithful Susan unmarried, and lost no time in renewing his suit.

In four weeks Susan became Mrs. Bickford, her husband became the owner of the farm he coveted, and he at once took his place among the prominent men of Pumpkin Hollow.

We now turn to Joe.

Since his departure nothing definite had been heard of him. Another boy had taken his place on Major Norton's farm, but he was less reliable than Joe.

One day Major Norton said:

JOE'S LUCK

"I am out of patience with that boy. I wish I had Joe back again."

At this moment a knock was heard at the door, and just afterward Joe entered.

He wore a mixed suit considerably the worse for wear and patched in two or three places. There was a rip under the arm, and his hat, a soft felt one, had become shapeless from long and apparently hard usage. He stood in the door-way waiting for recognition.

"How do you do, Joe?" said Major Norton, cordially. "I am glad to see you."

"Thank you, sir," he said. "How do you do, Oscar?"

"I'm well," said Oscar. "Have you been to California?"

"Yes."

"You don't seem to have made your fortune."

"I haven't starved," said Joe.

"Where did you get that suit of clothes?" asked Oscar.

"I hope you'll excuse my appearance," said Joe.

"Well, Joe, do you want to come back to your old place?" asked Major Norton. "I've got a boy but he doesn't suit me."

"How much would you be willing to pay me?"

"I'll do the same by you, as before, and give you fifty cents a week besides."

"Thank you for the offer, Major Norton. I'll take till to-morrow to think of it. I am going to look about the village a little. I will call again."

After Joe went out Oscar said:

JOE'S LUCK

"It does me good to see Joe come in rags. Serves him right for putting on airs."

On the main street Joe met Annie Raymond.

"Why, Joe!" she exclaimed, delighted. "Is it really you?"

"Bad pennies always come back," said Joe.

"Have you—I am afraid you have not been fortunate," said the young lady, hesitating as she noticed Joe's shabby clothes.

"Do you think less of me for that?"

"No," said Annie Raymond, warmly. "It is you I like, not your clothes. You may have been unfortunate, but I am sure you deserved success."

"You are a true friend, Miss Annie, so I don't mind telling you that I was successful."

Annie Raymond looked astonished.

"And these clothes——" she began.

"I put on for Oscar Norton's benefit. I wanted to see how he would receive me. He evidently rejoiced at my bad fortune."

"Oscar is a mean boy. Joe, you must come to our house to supper."

"Thank you, I will; but I will go round to the hotel and change my clothes."

"Never mind."

"But I do mind. I don't fancy a shabby suit as long as I can afford to wear a good one."

Joe went to the hotel, took off his ragged clothes, put on a new and stylish suit which he recently had made for him, donned a gold watch and chain, and hat in the latest style, and thus dressed, his natural good looks were becomingly set off.

JOE'S LUCK

"How do I look now?" he asked when he met Miss Annie Raymond at her own door.

"Splendidly, Joe. I thought you were a young swell from the city."

After supper Annie said, her eyes sparkling with mischief:

"Suppose we walk over to Major Norton's and see Oscar?"

"Just what I wanted to propose."

Oscar was out in the front yard, when he caught sight of Joe and Annie Raymond approaching. He did not at first recognize Joe, but thought, like the young lady, that it was some swell from the city.

"I thought you were poor," he muttered at last.

"I have had better luck than you thought."

"I suppose you spent all your money for those clothes?"

"You are mistaken, Oscar. I am not so foolish. I left between two and three thousand dollars in a New York bank, and I have more than twice that in San Francisco."

"I don't understand it. How did you do it?"

"I suppose it was my luck," said Joe.

"Not wholly that," said Annie Raymond. "It was luck and labor."

"I accept the amendment, Miss Annie."

Oscar's manner changed at once. Joe, the successful California miner, was very different from Joe, the hired boy. He became very attentive to our hero, and before he left town condescended to borrow twenty dollars of him, which he never remembered to repay. He wanted to go back to California with

JOE'S LUCK

Joe, but to this Oscar's father would not consent.

When Joe returned to San Francisco, by advice of Mr. Morgan, he sold out his restaurant to Watson and took charge of the latter's real estate business. He rose with the rising city, became a very rich man, and now lives in a handsome residence on one of the hills that overlook the bay. He has an excellent wife—our old friend, Annie Raymond—and a fine family of children. His domestic happiness is by no means the smallest part of Joe's luck.

THE END

Other books by
James Stevenson Publisher
For Children:
California History for Children
California Missions, History and Model Building Ideas for Children
California's Beginnings, A Children's Reader
For Adults:
The Capital That Couldn't Stay Put (Award winner, Calif's capitals)
Napa Valley's Natives -Monograph, by Richard Dillon
Six Months in the Gold Mines - Bancroft extremely complimentary...
Spanish Hill, Gold Hill, **The California Mining Country**
The Life of Mrs. Robert Louis Stevenson (Biography) and others...

Printed in the United States
21221LVS00001B/209